THE GREATEST HEIST IN JOVIALA

ALSO BY ADI ALSAID

The Bravest Warrior in Nefaria

THE GREATEST HEIST IN JOVIALA

ADI ALSAID

ALADDIN
NEW YORK   LONDON   TORONTO   SYDNEY   NEW DELHI

This book is a work of fiction. Any references to historical events, real people, or real places are used fictitiously. Other names, characters, places, and events are products of the author's imagination, and any resemblance to actual events or places or persons, living or dead, is entirely coincidental.

ALADDIN

An imprint of Simon & Schuster Children's Publishing Division

1230 Avenue of the Americas, New York, New York 10020

First Aladdin hardcover edition November 2024

Text copyright © 2024 by Adi Alsaid

Jacket illustration copyright © 2024 by Kristina Kister

All rights reserved, including the right of reproduction in whole or in part in any form.

ALADDIN and related logo are registered trademarks of Simon & Schuster, LLC.

Simon & Schuster: Celebrating 100 Years of Publishing in 2024

For information about special discounts for bulk purchases, please contact Simon & Schuster Special Sales at 1-866-506-1949 or business@simonandschuster.com.

The Simon & Schuster Speakers Bureau can bring authors to your live event. For more information or to book an event contact the Simon & Schuster Speakers Bureau at 1-866-248-3049 or visit our website at www.simonspeakers.com.

Book designed by Laura Lyn DiSiena and Irene Vandervoort

The text of this book was set in New Aster LT.

Manufactured in the United States of America 1024 BVG

10 9 8 7 6 5 4 3 2 1

Library of Congress Cataloging-in-Publication Data

Names: Alsaid, Adi, author.

Title: The greatest heist in Joviala / Adi Alsaid.

Description: First Aladdin hardcover edition. | New York : Aladdin, 2024. | Audience: Ages 8 to 12. | Summary: Candelabra's sister is trapped in a painting, and nothing in the kingdom Nefaria has helped—but the most powerful magic object in the world is in disaster-prone Joviala, and that is where Candelabra and the other exchange students are headed.

Identifiers: LCCN 2024010736 (print) | LCCN 2024010737 (ebook) | ISBN 9781665927789 (hc) | ISBN 9781665927802 (ebook)

Subjects: LCSH: Theft—Juvenile fiction. | Magic—Juvenile fiction. | Blessing and cursing—Juvenile fiction. | Sisters—Juvenile fiction. | Friendship—Juvenile fiction. | CYAC: Stealing—Fiction. | Magic—Fiction. | Blessing and cursing–Fiction. | Sisters—Fiction. | Friendship—Fiction.

Classification: LCC PZ7.1.A475 Gr 2024 (print) | LCC PZ7.1.A475 (ebook) | DDC [Fic]—dc23

LC record available at https://lccn.loc.gov/2024010736

LC ebook record available at https://lccn.loc.gov/2024010737

This is for The Freeze

1

THE PEOPLE IN THE KINGDOM OF JOVIALA HAD VERY STRONG fingers. They knew how to hold on better than anyone else, they liked to say. Mostly to the things that brought them joy.

They were experts at swinging from monkey bars, and at flying kites, and at holding hands. They never lost their grip on the reins of their horses, splinters were easily pulled out, and almost every person around gave great massages. The Jovialese could flick boogers from one edge of a field to another, which was enough to bring joy to all the kids in the kingdom—and some adults, too. They were expert rock climbers, and on any given weekend dozens of people could be spotted on the face of Mount Saint Helenhunt, scampering their way up to the dormant crater. Jovialese knights never lost their swords (not that they ever went to war), and their wizards never lost their wands, and these were some of the many reasons why Joviala was a happy kingdom, even if it often experienced disasters. Those strong, happy fingers also helped the people of Joviala hold on during times of high winds, and during earthquakes, and when flooding rivers threatened to carry them away.

They were known throughout many kingdoms to hold on to all sorts of other things too: traditions, the past, grudges.

At least that was what Candelabra was learning from her homeroom teacher in the adjacent Kingdom of Nefaria. Nefaria was a very different place: beautiful, and generally free from natural disasters, but prone to evil schemes.

Candelabra and a few of her friends were among those who had been selected for a student-exchange program in Joviala. They were going to embark on a weeklong trip to their northern neighbor, and they had been learning a lot about the land. To Candelabra, though, there seemed to be a lot of her teacher's opinions mixed into the lessons.

"And, sure, maybe there are no evil schemes there," Mr. Gigglebutt said, rubbing his hands together and creating a cloud of chalk dust. "But trust me, it's not such a great place. I've been, and it smells kind of fishy to me."

"Didn't you take the sixth graders last year to a fish market there?" Candelabra asked, not bothering to raise her hand.

Mr. Gigglebutt waved away the chalk dust and pretended not to hear the question. "But since we *are* going and the school insists on it, remember that your essays on your favorite bit about Joviala that we've covered in class are due the morning *before* we leave." Everyone in the classroom groaned, except for Candelabra's friend Bobert, who'd probably already written his. "You can write about anything at all—don't complain! It can be about their disasters, their history, or even about the fishy smell they have. Although I'm sure most of you will write about the Muffin of Glory," he said derisively.

Candelabra herself had chosen that topic. After all, Joviala being home to the most powerful known magical object was pretty cool.

The bell rang, and most students gathered their belongings and roared out of the classroom. Bobert waited by Candelabra's desk, like he usually did. Bobert seemed to always be happy to wait for Candelabra, even though he liked being on time to everything, and Candelabra didn't like to rush. Even the year before, when they'd finally broken free of the spell of an evil wizard (it was a long story), Candelabra hadn't run out of the castle with all the other kids. She'd taken her time leaving, running her fingers along the stone wall as if saying goodbye to a place she loved, not a royal home where she'd been imprisoned. Bobert had been right there with her, even though he was the one who had been trapped the longest, and all because of her.

Candelabra and Bobert were the last two to push open the

school's big wooden doors and emerge from the stone building into the sunny afternoon. Other kids were chatting excitedly, playing frees-bees, or running through the field toward the woods (ignoring the frustrated pleas of teachers to stay on school grounds until someone signed them out, which was a new security addition after Bobert's disappearance the year before). Candelabra waved to their friends Jennizabeth and Stanbert, who were boarding the carriage to go home.

"Remember your snacks!" Jennizabeth called out. They'd made a pact to bring various goodies to share for the long journey to Joviala. Bobert gave her a thumbs-up. He was going to bring some of his dad's flying goat jerky. It wasn't made from the flying goats that were constantly overhead in Nefaria, but from regular goats. The jerky just happened to fly. Candelabra waved, though she wasn't in the mood to think about snacks.

Her mind was on something a little more substantial. Something more permanent.

They kept walking around the main building. Often at this point they'd be debriefing about the school day, checking in on whether they'd noticed anything that could hint at an evil scheme. Mostly they'd be joking about one thing or another, which was what Candelabra often thought was her favorite part of friendship. The ability to talk about nothing and make it fun. Today, though, Candelabra was distracted, deep in her own thoughts.

THE GREATEST HEIST IN JOVIALA

Once they had signed out of school, they continued on their usual path home—they lived in the same area on the outskirts of town—heading past the school's various pigpens, following the shadow of the turret on the berry fields. When they were nearing the spider-monkey snack shack, Bobert turned to Candelabra. "Are you excited for the trip?"

Candelabra was running her hands along one of her braids. She wasn't listening, so Bobert gave her some space and walked quietly beside her through the woods on their way to town.

They stopped at the snack shack and perused the day's selections. When they paid the spider monkey running the shack for Candelabra's swampmallows and Bobert's painted chips, Candelabra whispered, so quietly that Bobert wasn't sure she'd even spoken, "Very."

Bobert frowned. "Really?"

"You're not excited to go?" she said, wondering what her face was doing.

"I am. I just didn't think you were. You've been quiet." He gave a little shrug. He didn't really mind if she felt like being quiet. He had been the king of quiet for a long time.

She popped a swampmallow in her mouth and chewed thoughtfully as they continued down the path.

"Then what are you going to write for the essay? What are you most excited about?" Bobert asked.

"Oh, probably listening to Mr. Gigglebutt complain for

a whole week," she deadpanned. Why Mr. Gigglebutt had accepted a role as chaperone for the weeklong trip to Joviala despite his clear distaste for it was a mystery they hadn't yet solved. "What about you?"

Bobert laughed. "I guess just seeing somewhere new. And not having to worry about evil schemes will be pretty cool too."

"I hadn't thought of that," Candelabra said, though this was a lie. "Do you really think they don't have any at all there? That people are just happy all the time?"

"It's kind of hard to believe, right?" Bobert responded. "But I'm excited to find out. And also to see what kinds of things they snack on!"

"Have you ever gone to another land?" Candelabra asked, reaching up to swat at some leaves overhead. It was the time of year when everything was green and lovely, the weather so perfect you didn't even want to be inside except to sleep.

"Nope. You?"

"When I was little. Before my sister got, you know." She gestured with one hand, and Bobert nodded. Candelabra always felt uncomfortable bringing up her sister, who had been evil-schemed into a painting, where she was still stuck. It was a normal part of Candelabra's life, and she wanted everyone to treat her normally despite having her only caregiver stuck in a landscape. Except that as soon as she started talking about Sandraliere, no one knew how to act around her. "I don't remember a lot from it, though. We went to the Banana Republic. I remember the beach and eating fruit and mostly spending so much time in the sun that I felt sick one of the days."

"I didn't even know the sun could make you sick," Bobert said, taking a turn trying to reach the leaves. They arrived at the clearing through which they could see the town below, set in one of Nefaria's many valleys, surrounded by huge mountains. This was one of Candelabra's favorite views. Not just because it was beautiful, but because usually she was in the company of others when she came to it.

"That's one of the things about growing up," Candelabra said, taking her backpack off so that she could hold it in front of her. "You find out that more and more things can make you sick."

Bobert seemed to consider this for a second as he pulled off his own backpack and tossed it down the hill. "I don't know. I actually used to be a lot more scared of the world."

"And now?"

Candelabra was staring at him. She didn't know why she felt so serious all of a sudden. It was like she needed his answer to confirm that it was okay to not be so scared of the world. She was hopeful about this upcoming trip for several reasons, but she didn't know if the hope was warranted, or if she even had the right to feel hope. Instead of answering, though, Bobert gave her a big smile and then threw himself down the hill.

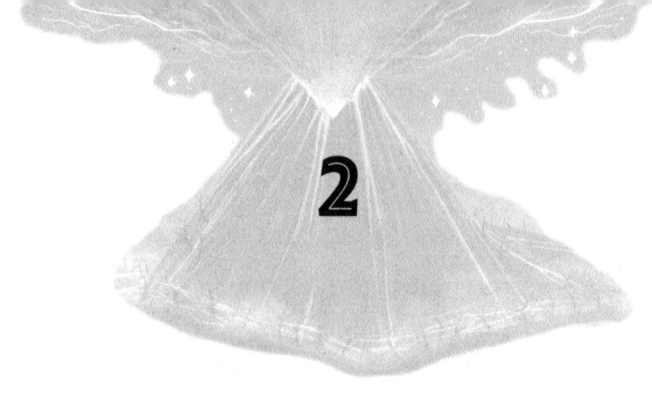

2

CANDELABRA WAS AN EXPERT HILL ROLLER. WHEN IT came to the hill that every kid in Nefaria rolled down (no exceptions), some thought you just had to go fast, but in her opinion the perfect hill roll was smooth and lasted as long as possible. She took this route home every day, and she'd been tinkering with her technique since she came of school age. So while Bobert raced ahead of her, she was contemplating their conversation while bracing for the familiar bumps and avoiding the rocks that no one had managed to disinter.

She thought about the nearly invisible boy Bobert used to be, and how he was now. And how that gave her hope for change.

If anyone thought it strange that Candelabra did some of her best thinking while rolling down the hill, then they clearly hadn't tried it. The smell of grass, the thrill of falling, the slight pain that made you feel alive, the disorienting view of sky flashing in and out of sight: all of it was perfect for thoughtfulness. And it was near the bottom of the hill when Candelabra had her epiphany. It had been building within her for the last few months, ever since the exchange program had been announced and she had decided to apply. It had been brewing for longer than that, probably. Things had changed irrevocably for Candelabra's little family once before. And that meant they could change again.

Candelabra was stuck in a repeating cycle of getting herself ready for school while her sister looked on from the painting, of coming home to sit in front of the frame and do her homework while her sister sunned herself beneath her always-blue sky. Candelabra had been cooking her own dinner, had been cleaning up after herself, had been assuring the neighbors she was okay, day in and day out for the past two years. And she was okay-ish. She knew better than to complain, in Nefaria of all places. But just because she was okay didn't mean she wanted things to stay the same.

Candelabra had tried all sorts of ways to free her sister, especially in the last year, taking advantage of the momentary celebrity brought to her and her friends for helping rescue the kingdom. No benevolent wizard had been able to break the spell; no artist had been able to paint a bridge for Sandraliere to reenter the world. She'd researched every potion available at the many apothecaries nearby, but none of them had worked.

There were still a few items with potential: a book written

by a famous witch with spells that could break any curse, but there was only one copy, and it had been heavily damaged in a fire. Then there was lasagnanite, an extremely powerful magical mineral. But it was rare, and none of it had been found in Nefaria for hundreds of years.

But tomorrow Candelabra was going to leave Nefaria. She was going to arrive in a place that had no evil schemes, which maybe meant it was exactly the kind of place that could help her. Maybe this trip to Joviala wasn't just a school-sponsored outing to learn about a different land. Maybe one of those supposedly strong-fingered Jovialese would know how to get Sandraliere out of that painting. Maybe they could just reach in and use their strong hands to pull her out.

Candelabra came to a stop at the bottom of the hill, where Bobert was brushing himself off and smiling from ear to ear. "That was a good one," he said. "You wanna go again?"

She stayed on her back, taking in the realization she'd come to: that Joviala could offer a whole new slew of solutions for her to test out. Suddenly, the excitement she'd been feeling for the trip—based solely on the fact that it would bring a change to her routine—felt uncontainable. Even though climbing up the hill and rolling down it again didn't appeal to her all that much—there was nothing new there, after all—she sprang to her feet, energy coursing through her. Change was possible.

That night, her usual dinner of monster-bone broth and raw carrots tasted a little better than it had the previous seven hundred nights or so. (Okay, she was exaggerating. Sometimes neighbors brought over casseroles, or Sandraliere let her dip into their savings to order scorpion pizza.) She sat cross-legged in front of the fire she'd built, directly below her sister's painting, which was hanging over the mantel. She slurped happily, putting the finishing touches on her essay as she ate.

"What are you so smiley about?" her sister called out. Usually, Candelabra was thankful that she could at least talk to her sister. She would have liked to have touch available for the occasional hug, or so that her sister could help do the dishes every now and then. But again, Nefarians learned to be thankful for a lot. Right now, though, her reaction was to roll her eyes.

"I'm not smiley."

"I can see your teeth."

"Because I'm eating!"

"No, those are smile teeth, not food teeth." Sandraliere bit into one of the apples from the tree near her cottage. She was sitting at the edge of the prairie closest to the frame of the painting, so she could see Candelabra. She'd probably eaten the same apple hundreds of times. She said they tasted just like real apples, even though they were made from paint and reappeared as soon as she'd picked them. Now she had one of those big stupid grins she got when she thought she was being funny. "They're all the same teeth," Candelabra grumbled.

"We might be living in separate worlds, kid, but I still know when you're happy."

Candelabra bit into a carrot as loudly as she could, averting her eyes. She heard Sandraliere get closer to the edge of the painting. "Candy, you're allowed to be excited about going on a trip, you know."

"I know."

"Okay, then why are you being so weird?" Candelabra held her bowl up to her face and made a point of slurping down the rest of her broth. "Fine, be that way," Sandraliere said. She retreated to the lounge chair she'd found somewhere in her painted world and had dragged to the front of the frame. "You're all packed? You did your assignments for the week?"

"Yes, *Mom*." Candelabra stood and moved toward the kitchen, hiding her smile as she said it. Sandraliere basically *was* her mom. She'd been taking care of Candelabra for almost as long as she could remember. But Sandraliere had been old enough when their actual parents had died that she felt weird about being called that; she wanted to be the cool older sister and not the stand-in parent. So it was the only surefire way Candelabra had to annoy her sister when she was being annoying.

THE GREATEST HEIST IN JOVIALA

"Keep it up and I'll ground you!" her sister said, her voice carrying over with the slight breeze that was always blowing from the painting.

"I'd like to see you try!" She plopped her dishes into the sink and ran water over them, deciding she'd wash them properly in the morning before heading to school. Sandraliere always slept in during the mornings, and Candelabra wanted to spend as much time with her sister as she could before she left. The longest she'd been away from her since the whole curse thing happened had been just a couple of weeks, and that was during the gumball-machine curse that Bobert fell into.

Back in front of the fire, she curled up on the rocking chair with her favorite blanket to read more about Joviala on her wizard tablet. It used a magical, invisible network of signals in the air that allowed her to look up practically anything she wanted.

She tried to keep all her teeth completely hidden, stealing a quick glance up at Sandraliere, who was openly smirking.

"What?" Candelabra asked.

"Nothing."

They sat quietly together for a while, even though they weren't really together. Candelabra read about the land she was going to visit, and Sandraliere read a paperback novel that Candelabra had been able to throw into the painting. Two years into their whole ordeal, they were still trying to understand a lot of the rules of how the spell that kept her affixed to the wall worked. Food regrew, and some items could make it through the painting if Candelabra threw hard enough and aimed at the perfect spot. Almost everything else was a question mark. They couldn't even tell if Sandraliere was aging or not.

It was a lovely evening, all things considered, and it was made all the sweeter by the thought that soon everything could change.

3

NOTHING MADE SHMEBECCA FERGUSON HAPPIER THAN squatting in the dirt on the slopes of Mount Saint Helenhunt and trying to figure out what she was looking at.

Everyone else looked at the mountain and just saw something big. It was the tallest peak in Joviala, with the largest trees, and the biggest crater at the top. But Shmebecca was more interested in all the tiny, fascinating things she could find on the ground there. All the different minerals that sparkled with subtle colors within the rocks. The types of rocks themselves, and how they told the story of Mount Saint Helenhunt's long and explosive life.

The volcano was dormant now, but it hadn't always been. And it probably wouldn't be forever, though no one knew when or how it would wake up. Some mountains woke up gently, and others were like Shmebecca's little brothers, twins Shmorris and Shborris, who never got out of bed without screaming for at least twenty minutes or throwing at least four things. That was why they didn't own anything made of glass anymore.

Shmebecca shifted through a pile of pebbles, hoping to find a few more pieces for her mosaic of Mount Saint Helenhunt erupting in the night sky. She had plenty of glassy black obsidian for the background, but she needed more rocks that were rich with silica and could recreate the pretty pink and gold streaks that made Mount Saint Helenhunt the most beautiful mountain around. The mosaic had started as an art project for school, but she hadn't had the time to finish it properly, and now it had simply become the thing she thought about all the time. Well, other than the mountain itself.

Her classmates didn't get it—or, really, get *her*—but it didn't matter. She'd rather be here, smelling the subtle, earthy odors of the mountain, than playing sock-hair with the other kids. What could be more boring than chasing a sock full of hair around a grass field for an hour? Here was geological history *in the palm of her hand*. The colors of ancient minerals told the story of explosions and solidification, of gases and fire and ash meeting the air. At any moment she could find something that no one else had, unearth some clue as to when or if Mount Saint Helenhunt would wake up again. Even if it seemed like no one else around her cared.

Shmebecca's own history was written into that mountain

too. Though, maybe it was more accurate to say she would have *been* history if not for the mountain.

The first thought she had when she saw the pebbles around her start trembling was that a herd of mammoth rabbits was scampering up or down the slopes, or a giant rat-bird had fallen asleep on a tree branch and thudded down to the ground. Or perhaps there was a tour group or field trip taking place, with kids running around, happy to be outside, not really understanding much of the power and the beauty that they were stomping around on.

But then Shmebecca looked around and saw none of the usual suspects. No rabbits, no rat-birds, no kids. She was rather alone, except for the old couple on the other side of the grassy plain who had set up portable stools to look at wildlife. She sat still for a moment (or, rather, squatted still) and tried to suss out what she had just seen, if she had really seen anything at all.

Then she saw the pebbles dance again.

She sniffed the air, expecting to smell sulfur, which was common in volcanic eruptions—even just small releases of gas and vapor, which Shmebecca thought were more likely with what she called *her* mountain than some huge explosion. Instead she just smelled the usual pleasant odors of the grass and the fresh air, the flowers in the plain.

The bird watchers hadn't even seemed to notice the shaking. Shmebecca looked up at the trees. Animals were much better at sensing natural disasters than people were. But the two giant rat-birds perched on a high branch barely ruffled their feathers. There were no hordes of deer or wildebeests or slug-people fleeing to safety.

Disappointment was probably not the first emotion she should have been feeling. But she huffed a sigh and walked over to the nearby trail. Maybe from the clearing she'd be able to see a plume of smoke coming from the crater, and then the next few weeks would be extremely exciting. The kingdom's top volcanologists would probably arrive to take samples and run tests, and she could offer to carry stuff for them or get them some goods from her mom's bakery and use that as an excuse to ask them each millions of questions.

When she got to the clearing, she didn't notice anything different. But down in the valley she saw something that caught her eye. Not the confetti cannons that were going off in town—that was a usual occurrence, since Jovialese liked celebrating every little thing. No, closer to Shmebecca, at the foothills of Mount Saint Helenhunt, a whole lot of activity was going on: Men wearing hats (mostly top hats, even though it seemed to be a construction site) were carrying shovels. There'd been a track built that extended all the way to town, from what she could tell, and on that track were large digging machines, the kind used in construction. Straight below, some scaffolding had already been set up along a cliff wall.

Shmebecca frowned. Then she heard a whistle, followed by some yelling. The men all stopped moving, and she thought she saw them cover their ears. Then there was a muffled boom, and Shmebecca felt the ground shaking again. A puff of smoke rose from below, making her cough. She didn't bother going back to peek over the edge at what they were doing. She was going down there to get a closer look.

4

SHMEBECCA ARRIVED AT THE APPARENT CONSTRUCTION site a sweaty mess. Her cheeks were flushed and her ponytail had come seventy percent undone, with more dark hair sticking up every which way than was contained in the flimsy hair tie. Not bothering to compose herself, Shmebecca huffed around, ignoring the passing looks of the builders and the diggers. She was looking for someone in charge. Some lady wearing a monocle, probably, or a guy with a cane who liked to twirl his mustache.

At the very least she wanted to come across someone in scientist robes, or in adequate gear to explore a crater. She wasn't sure how this whole operation had gotten past her. Who knew how long they'd been setting up for. She supposed there was no good way to approach the mountain from that side. It was mostly cliff walls and flying-goat caves. Still, she was embarrassed that she'd been unaware of this big happening on her mountain, but it would be much better if the surprise operation were at least a scientific one. Then she could maybe tag along, or at least talk to someone about the more interesting parts of the mountain.

"Why hello there, little one!" a big guy in overalls said as he stepped in front of her. "You should be careful. There's a lot of dangerous tools around and explosions and such." He pointed at a rake that for some reason had been left on the ground with the pointy parts up, then at another worker, who was juggling knives.

Shmebecca crossed her arms. "What is this?"

The man frowned but didn't stop smiling (an impressive feat of facial muscles). "Well, I suppose this was a friendly warning from an adult feeling a certain sense of responsibility upon seeing a young girl potentially hurt herself?"

Shmebecca rolled her eyes, then gestured at the hubbub all around them. "I meant *this*. You people. The . . . tools. Why are there tools and digging machines? And why do you not have tiltmeters or gas-sample jars or even a wizard to cast a thermal-imaging spell?"

"Those are all big words for such a little person!" The man laughed heartily, putting his whole belly into it.

"Who's in charge here?" Shmebecca asked, before her eyes could roll themselves out of her head.

The man truly frowned now, looking a little hurt that Shmebecca wasn't laughing along with him. Her mom always told her that other people didn't appreciate her eye rolls very much, but she couldn't resist. "Well, I suppose that would be Mr. Eyebrows," he said, looking in the direction of a man wearing a colorful cape and carrying a clipboard in a very official manner. He was talking to a woman with frizzy hair and a man with a traditional yellow hard hat, and all of them were pointing at the mountain. At *her* mountain.

"Why do you call him Mr. Eyebrows? Actually—never mind." If Eyebrows was in charge, she decided to just go ask him what was going on.

Shmebecca turned away from the jolly construction worker. Thankfully, marching through a construction zone as an eleven-year-old was easier in Joviala than it was in many other kingdoms. Bad things didn't really happen in Joviala. At least not like they did in other kingdoms. They didn't happen *on purpose*.

Sure, Joviala had its fair share of natural disasters. Other volcanoes in the Gee Golly mountain range had erupted violently, and earthquakes were pretty common. There was also fire-tornado season, and snake thunder (which was Shmebecca's least favorite). And accidents happened, of course, just like everywhere else. Shmebecca knew that better than anyone.

She'd been eight years old when her family had gone to Mount Saint Helenhunt for a picnic. Her brothers had been nonstop motion machines, little giggling gobs of flesh with legs that never got tired of pumping forward. Her parents had had to chase them around all day, leaving Shmebecca to roam on her own, looking for bugs, as was her hobby at the time.

She'd spotted a rare gentleman bug with a beautiful top hat and monocle saying "excuse me" as it maneuvered through the grass. Having never seen one in the wild before, and since her parents were busy with Shmorris and Shborris, Shmebecca followed it for a long time, just watching its silly little gait, appreciating the fact that nature could come up with such a polite creature.

She'd followed the bug through the plain, into the woods, and toward the hot mud springs, barely pausing to think about how far she was getting from the picnic site. By the time she tripped over the water pump hidden in the bushes, it was too late.

She learned later that the water pump shouldn't have been there. But there it was, and it sent her sprawling into the hot springs.

The mud famously had healing properties if you stuck your feet in, but it was thick and heavy like the best kind of milkshakes and the worst kind of baths. Like a bath, the mud was hot, and Shmebecca had gone into it face-first. With her arms in the mud too, she struggled to get out. She squirmed, trying to stay calm but feeling her breath run out.

If it weren't for the coincidence that the mountain emitted

a rare gastric exhalation (a mountain burp), not uncommon in dormant volcanoes, Shmebecca would have very likely drowned in that mud. But the mountain *did* burp, and the bubble of volcanic gas shot Shmebecca right back out of the hot mud spring, saving her life.

That mishap with the water pump, however, had been an accident. The Fun Corporation, which was exploring a project on the mountain, was simply trying to be a little more efficient—they told their workers to save time by not putting away their equipment. Had they known that leaving their equipment out might send people flying into hot mud springs, they wouldn't have done it. Not in Joviala. People didn't cause each other harm here, not intentionally. There was very little wrongdoing in general.

That didn't necessarily mean adults inherently trusted or liked children. But children were usually allowed to run around as they pleased. Which was why no one stopped Shmebecca as she crossed the construction site to tug on Mr. Eyebrows's cape while he was in the middle of a sentence.

". . . as you see here on these very technical charts, we'll just—" He looked down at Shmebecca. He did have a mustache, but not a very twirlable one. And his eyebrows were slightly bushy but not notably so. He looked like one of her classmates' dads. Maybe one of the rich ones. "Oh wow, a child!" he exclaimed. "Yes, tiny person?" He made eye contact with the adults he'd been explaining stuff to. "Why is one of these here?" He had an unsettling smile, too big and too empty all at the same time.

"That's exactly what I wanted to ask you. What are you doing here?"

"You don't know?" He looked to the frizzy-haired woman standing next to him. "Are there people who don't know? This isn't a secret, right?"

The woman looked down at her own clipboard and shook her head very aggressively. "No, sir, according to our notes, everyone in the kingdom should know. I'll have Shmelinda write up another six to seven press releases." She pulled a carrier pigeon out of her jacket pocket, tied a little note to its feet, and then gave it a light spank, which caused it to take off with a coo and a flutter of wings.

Mr. Eyebrows went back to talking to the frizzy-haired woman and the man with the yellow hard hat. They seemed to have forgotten about her.

"Anyway, once we set off the next four boom-booms we should be able to—"

"What is going on here!" Shmebecca shouted.

Mr. Eyebrows once again looked surprised to see her down there. "You still don't know?" He chuckled. "Why, we—that is, the Fun Corporation, with me at the helm—are moving the mountain, of course!"

5

AFTER AN ALL-DAY JOURNEY UP THE WIGGLY-SHMIGGLY River, Bobert and Candelabra, along with their friends Stanbert and Jennizabeth, carried their belongings off the boat, tired, dazed, and a little giddy. Bobert could tell right away that Joviala was a beautiful place, surrounded by mountains similar to ones in Nefaria, even though they felt a little more welcoming, somehow.

The air was perfectly pleasant, not hot or muggy, the slightest breeze caressing his cheeks in a way that reminded him of his dad's beard brushing against him when he leaned over Bobert's bed to kiss him good night. The weather had been lovely when they left Nefaria, but here things were even lovelier.

Ever since he'd escaped Matt the Evil Wizard's castle the year before, Bobert had been completely happy, and he didn't want anything at all to change.

"Wait, why is the sun still out?" Stanbert asked no one in

particular. "Isn't it almost nighttime?" Stanbert squinted up at the bright blue sky and almost walked off the boat into the river.

The muscular arms of Imogene Petunias came to the rescue, though, grabbing him by his backpack and lifting him straight up in the air before he could embarrass—and soak—himself. "Aren't they teaching you kids any science at all?" she asked.

Imogene Petunias was kind of a mystery to Bobert and the others at school. She'd been there last year when the spell had been broken, and now she sometimes volunteered at the school for special events. But she didn't seem like a teacher at all, and as far as Bobert knew, she wasn't anyone's relative. She liked to say that she was enjoying her retirement with the kids, but no one knew what she had retired *from*.

She actually seemed most interested in Bobert himself, which he wasn't about to start questioning, since it made him a lot cooler in everyone's eyes. Cooler than even he felt he was.

Mr. Gigglebutt, who was chaperoning along with Miss Petunias, muttered something about how they'd covered Joviala's sunniness in class, but at that point the kids were a little too excited to care to be reminded that it was because of the kingdom being a little farther north and a lot more charmed than Nefaria.

Bobert hefted his duffel bag and followed his friends off

the boat. When he stepped on the wooden dock, he looked excitedly up at Candelabra. "My first step in a new kingdom!" At her smile he said, "I don't really feel any different."

She laughed. "Yeah, well, give it a second."

Mr. Gigglebutt led them over to talk to the welcoming party of staff and parents from the Jovialese school. It was a little alarming to the Nefarians when the locals—who were holding signs that said things like WELCOME TO THE HAPPIEST KINGDOM IN THE WORLD! and WE'RE SO GLAD YOU'RE HERE!—threw tiny colored pieces of paper at them and sang a welcome song at full volume, but that was mostly because Nefarians were used to aggressive strangers. They were going to have to tamp down their suspicions while here. Finally, when the awkward hello was over, Mr. Gigglebutt led the kids to their separate host families, and Bobert really took in the sight of the welcoming committee.

All of them were smiling from ear to ear, and not a single one of those smiles looked forced. For a brief moment Bobert was a little weirded out by this, thinking that surely one of these kids was angry about having to share their room with strangers from a strange land. Maybe some of them were planning on pranking the kids from Nefaria. Maybe whoever Bobert was going to stay with would make him do their chores, or their homework, or their hair.

But if everything he'd read about Joviala was to be believed, then they wouldn't do that. They were going to be perfectly sweet. He shook the thought away and tuned in just in time to hear Mr. Gigglebutt introduce Bobert and Candelabra to their host family: the Fergusons.

The parents, a tall woman named Shmary and a short, stout man named Shmarcos, greeted Bobert and Candelabra with even bigger smiles. They would have been almost scary if they hadn't seemed so sincere. "We are so happy to have you!" Shmarcos said. "We are huggers, if you ever want one, but no pressure. These are the twins, Shmorris and Shborris." He put a hand on the shoulders of the two smiling boys, who seemed to be about six years old. "Our daughter, Shmebecca, was supposed to be here, but she's probably on the mountain somewhere."

He punctuated this with a loud laugh, as if Bobert and Candelabra would get the joke. They shared a look with each other, but Shmary and the twins didn't laugh either, so maybe he was just one of those adults who laughed at himself even when he wasn't funny.

"Don't mind him," Shmary said. "He laughs a lot at things that aren't funny. Mostly himself."

"Too true!" Shmarcos said, laughing again.

"I imagine you're hungry and tired. We can take the shortcut home, if you prefer. Or, if you're feeling up for it, we can go to our favorite restaurant. It's some of the best local cuisine, plus we should get a lovely view of the sunset. Totally up to you, though!"

"No pressure, but you should pick the restaurant," Shmorris said, revealing a gap where his two front teeth would have been. Or was he Shborris? "They have the best desserts, and we can usually talk Ma and Pa into getting us one of each. Especially if we have visitors!"

That's a scheme! Bobert thought. *Maybe not an evil one, but still.* But rather than squat down to give the boy a talking-to about being manipulative, or maybe even rolling their eyes and saying, "Nice try," the Fergusons let out a hearty chuckle, together this time.

"That's true!" Shmary said, and Shmarcos ruffled his son's hair.

Bobert looked at Candelabra, raising his eyebrow. But she didn't return his look. Her eyes were glued to the Fergusons, a smile spreading across her lips.

The Fergusons treated Bobert and Candelabra to one of the best meals either of them had ever had. Fried fish with garlic and chili, fragrant coconut rice, a handful of different salads so packed with flavor that Bobert had to wonder if everyone in Nefaria had completely misunderstood the idea of salads and what they could be. There were noodle soups where the noodles didn't come alive and try to kill you, and a dessert of ice cream and all these colorful jellies packed with flavor and fun! Sure, the claim sounded like an advertisement for the dessert, but it was true.

The view from their table had been beautiful, with Mount Saint Helenhunt directly in front of them, snowcapped and picturesque, and the clouds were streaked with color as the sun set. The Fergusons made Bobert and Candelabra the center of attention too, asking questions about life back in Nefaria, the conversation taking detours in the form of jokes and hypotheticals that had them all laughing until their sides hurt.

It almost made Bobert feel guilty that he was having such a good time without his parents. Then he thought about coming with them to visit Joviala, and the idea of doing that at some point in the future made the evening all the more enjoyable. He hadn't believed all the stuff about people in Joviala being so happy, but it was true. He could feel a sense of ease settling into his bones, a sense of calm that he didn't know he'd been missing. Candelabra, too, seemed more relaxed, and at the same time livelier.

Then it all stopped.

Shmebecca Ferguson stormed into the restaurant as if she'd known all along where they were. She barely acknowledged Bobert and Candelabra as she took the empty seat that they'd saved for her. Her cheeks were bright red, she was sweaty, and her dark hair was sticking to her forehead at the same time that it seemed to be trying to escape from her head altogether.

Shmary scooted a little closer and put her hand on her daughter's cheek. "Oh, honey. Do you want to talk about what's troubling you?"

Shmebecca was stuffing her mouth with too many forkfuls of food to answer, though. Bobert once again looked over at Candelabra to gauge her reaction, but she wasn't meeting his eye. She was staring at Shmebecca and chewing her bottom lip. He wondered what she was thinking about—if she was feeling guilty about being here, having a good time, without her sister. He wondered what it was like, having just one person in your family, and having that person stuck in a different world from you.

"Don't get me started," Shmebecca huffed, pulling Bobert from his thoughts. A little bit of rice shot out from her mouth and onto the table. She grabbed the grains with her fingers and swallowed them back down. Then she looked back and forth between Candelabra and Bobert. "You're the visitors, then?"

They both nodded, and Candelabra gave a little wave.

"Welcome," Shmebecca said dryly. Then, almost before she'd even finished saying the word, she followed it up with: "So, where you come from, people are always doing bad stuff that everyone else has to stop, right?"

"Honey!" Shmary exclaimed. "It's rude to—"

"No, it's okay," Candelabra said. "It's true." She shrugged. Now she finally looked at Bobert again, which calmed his old worries about being invisible. She was giving him room to tell his story about being stuck in the gumball machine if he wanted to, even though she'd been there for a lot of it too.

"It must be nice not having to worry about that," he said instead.

Shmary and Shmarcos looked down at their plates then, and the twins both started talking at the same time, repeating rumors they'd heard about things that had happened in Nefaria. Shmebecca, however, just narrowed her eyes and stared at Bobert as she took a forkful of salad and chewed thoughtfully.

Later that night Bobert was sitting with Candelabra in the twins' room, getting ready for bed. Shmorris and Shborris had been moved to their sister's room, a development that they seemed completely thrilled by and Shmebecca seemed indifferent to.

Candelabra pulled out her book and slid into the slightly too-small bed by the window. "So, now that you know what they snack on, are you ready to go back?"

Bobert laughed. "No! I would argue we know their meals, but we haven't seen any of their snacks. I think tomorrow I'm really going to make it a mission to try at least forty-seven different foods."

Candelabra laughed. "Yeah, this place is . . . something else."

"It's pretty cool," he admitted. "I wonder if we'll still feel that way when—"

He was interrupted by the door opening and Shmebecca storming inside, her hair still dripping wet from her shower. It seemed like storming was her preferred way to make an entrance.

She shut the door behind her, then turned to face them. "Okay, evil-scheme kids. I'm gonna need your help."

6

It took a second for Candelabra to process what Shmebecca had said. "That's not all we are," she said. It came out quieter than she wanted, not as combative as her usual self.

Shmebecca rolled her eyes. "Yeah, yeah, I'm sorry. I know that. But are you going to help or not?"

"Um. What do you need help with?" Bobert asked.

Shmebecca crossed her arms over her chest. Candelabra noticed how her eyes started filling with tears. Then her arms dropped to her sides, her face scrunched up, and she burst out crying.

Candelabra looked at Bobert, wondering what to do. He clearly didn't know either. He started to get up off the bed, but then stopped, one foot on the floor, his other knee still on the mattress.

"My mountain!" Shmebecca said in between sobs.

"Um," Bobert said again.

Candelabra approached the poor girl, wondering if she

should put a hand on her shoulder or hug her or what. She wished Sandraliere had given her an example of how to act in this situation, but providing physical comfort wasn't in the cards for them clearly, not anymore. So Candelabra opted to pat Shmebecca awkwardly on the back. "Hey there," she said, but then couldn't think of anything else, so she repeated it, as if those words could comfort anyone on their own.

It took twenty minutes for Shmebecca to compose herself enough to tell them what had happened.

But even then Shmebecca was speaking too quickly, saying a lot of details that Candelabra had no context for. Something about a fun corporation and a lot of details about the mountain that Candelabra wasn't sure were pertinent at the moment. But she really wanted to understand, wanted to help Shmebecca, if she could. "So, they want to move the mountain. Do you know where to?"

Shmebecca blinked. "Oh, I didn't even think of that! What if they move it really really far away, and I can never see it again?" This set off a whole new crying bout.

"Well, there are no evil schemes here, right?" Bobert said. They were all sitting on Shmorris's bed, Shmebecca in the middle. She'd been going through a lot of tissues, and Candelabra was a little worried that she would run out and use the bedsheet Candelabra was supposed to sleep on.

"I guess not," Shmebecca sniffled.

"So, it'll probably be okay. Maybe they're moving it for a good reason. Maybe they just need to move it a few inches."

Shmebecca shook her head. "Mr. Eyebrows said that they had to make way for a whole road. How big are roads? I feel like I don't even know. Are they this big?" She moved her hands about six inches apart. When Bobert and Candelabra didn't say anything right away, she kept increasing the distance between her palms asking, "This big?" every second or so with growing panic.

Candelabra reached out and gently grabbed Shmebecca's wrists, lowering her hands. "I don't think you can accurately depict the size of a road with your hands."

"Curses, I'm never going to see my mountain again." She lowered her head, but only for a second before snapping it back up. "You guys have to help me."

"We're just kids. What can we do against a construction project?" Bobert asked, his voice sounding small even to him. "We don't even know what kind of petitions to file with your Council of Elders."

"We don't have a Council of Elders in Joviala," Shmebecca sniffled.

Candelabra didn't think that would help much anyway, but it also wouldn't help to point that out, so she just stayed quiet. She felt bad for Shmebecca. Even in Nefaria, Candelabra would have had trouble thinking of a way to fix the problem. But that was if it was an evil scheme. In a land where evil schemes didn't exist, she wasn't sure if there *was* any recourse. Maybe the mountain needed to be moved for a legitimate reason. If it wasn't evil, it had to be okay, right?

A part of her wanted to dismiss Shmebecca's worries. To tell her that it would be all okay, so she could focus on being in this new land and search for a solution to an actual evil scheme.

But Shmebecca was her host sister, and if this had been Sandraliere asking for help, Candelabra wouldn't be giving up so easily. She had long ago resolved to be on the lookout for evil schemes. Not just ones affecting her. And even if this wasn't an evil scheme, it was hurting Shmebecca, and it could hurt others.

She didn't have to do just one or the other, after all. She could use her time in Joviala to find a way to break Sandraliere out of her painted prison, *and* she could help Shmebecca with her problem too.

"Okay, we'll help," she said. "At least we'll try."

"Really?" Shmebecca's smile lit up instantly. Over Shmebecca's shoulder, Candelabra saw Bobert frown. He probably knew it wasn't a great idea to promise to help when they had no clue if they could. But then that kind heart of his took over, and he nodded along. It was what she most admired about Bobert: he always put others first.

"We obviously can't promise anything," Candelabra continued. "But I think we have it in us to try to help. We've done harder things before." She widened her eyes suggestively at Bobert, who smirked.

"It's true," he said. "I think we'll be able to sneak around quite a bit tomorrow. They're giving us time to explore the grounds at the ruins. Plus, our chaperone is Mr. Gigglebutt, who barely knows where he is half the time."

Now Shmebecca giggled, wiping her eyes. She took a deep breath and sighed as if every single worry she had had been solved by Bobert and Candelabra's reassurance. She smoothed out the bedspread they were sitting on, even though doing so did nothing for the wrinkles.

It was a sort of magic, Candelabra thought. To be on a boat for a day and arrive somewhere new and then all of a sudden be able to sit in a stranger's house and make her feel better by just offering to help. What a shame that Sandraliere hadn't had the chance to do that for the last two years. She hadn't had the chance to make a new friend like Bobert, or to travel anywhere. Nothing new had happened to her sister in so long.

Before she could get too caught up in her thoughts, Shmary came by and said that it was time to go to bed. Shmebecca got up without any protest. She was about to walk out of the room, but then she turned around. "Thank you," she said. "This mountain . . . it's my whole world."

Candelabra nodded, looking deep into Shmebecca's eyes, thinking she knew what it was like to have your whole world be threatened. Even if she didn't fully believe Shmebecca's world really needed saving.

Candelabra would not have guessed that riding a bicycle early in the morning, almost entirely uphill, with a huge crowd around her, was something she'd enjoy. But she found herself smiling the whole way, despite her belief that people who chose to sweat in the morning had something seriously wrong with them.

It was a beautiful ride, and the weather was as great as it had been the day before—she was learning that things in Joviala could often be described in sweepingly positive terms. There was also the fun of just being somewhere new, doing something different! This was so different.

Her breakfast hadn't been the same bowl of bug cereal that she always had; it had been a big, heaping plate of pancakes and fresh fruit. She hadn't had to wave goodbye to her sister through a painting, hadn't had to avoid the poop bombs from flying goats on the walk to school. She'd had a pleasant stroll down a new path, with trees not entirely familiar to her, and flowers, and bugs whose minute movements caught her eye and made her slow down. Then, instead of arriving at school and wondering which of the jerks around her was planning to set a small fire in order to steal tests from a teacher's desk (or something), she had been surprised by the shiny bikes lent to the Nefarian kids by local students to make the journey to the ancient ruins easier.

Plus, there was the sheer possibility of this place. How many new things was she going to discover this week? The fact that she couldn't guess—even before factoring in trying to help Shmebecca save her mountain—made her giddy enough that she pedaled so fast she shot ahead to the front of the bike convoy.

Once they arrived, even though Mr. Gigglebutt was reading through a bunch of boring notes about the ruins they were visiting—notes he'd clearly prepared only the night before, if not that morning—Candelabra was still bouncing on her feet. The sun was in her eyes and she was probably going to be sweaty all day, but she didn't care. She was doing something new, somewhere new, and she wouldn't have it any other way.

Next to her, Bobert took notes in his notebook, or at least pretended to. She could see he was mostly doodling, and every now and then he'd realize he was doodling and try to pay attention again. Stanbert and Jennizabeth were passing a piece of paper back and forth, playing tic-tac-toe, which was a Nefarian game where you had to guess how many toes the other person had. It usually ended in a tie. The only kids who were paying attention were the Jovialese ones, who probably knew everything the Nefarian teacher was saying.

". . . is a hallmark of the ancient Jovialese, which you'll see on the engravings on many of the ruins at this site," Mr. Gigglebutt said. He was met with some laughter from the crowd, which was confusing to Candelabra.

"What was funny?" she asked Bobert.

"Apparently all their depictions of people have big butts," he said.

When the giggles had dissipated, Mr. Gigglebutt continued, addressing the four Nefarians directly. "Remember that you're not only here to learn about ancient people, but also ancient lands. There are stories to be told in these ruins, definitely, but there are even more stories in . . ." He paused, maybe for effect, or maybe because a stupid grin was spreading across his face. It happened every time he got to use the word in conversation or while teaching. "Rocks!" he exclaimed, and Candelabra heard Bobert say it with him half-heartedly.

"That's right," he continued, as if everyone were as excited as he was. "We're in volcanic land, after all, so you should be able to see a rich variety of igneous rocks. My students will want to take note of—or sketch, if possible—any evidence they see of a large-scale geologic event, such as . . ."

"I wonder if Shmebecca's mountain is a volcano," Candelabra said to Bobert.

THE GREATEST HEIST IN JOVIALA

"It is," he whispered back. "This is it." He gestured with his head at the mountain peak rising above them.

It seemed Candelabra had missed that bit of information while daydreaming. "Is that a good idea? To move a volcano?"

Bobert shrugged. "Maybe we can ask Mr. Gigglebutt."

"Hmm," Candelabra said.

Candelabra let her mind wander. She took note of the different colored rocks at her feet, and the weird butterflies with three sets of wings. In the distance she could hear a river, and it made her think of Sandraliere sitting by her creek alone, seeing the same thing day after day.

Once the teachers finished the lecture and gave the kids permission to explore, Candelabra and her group of friends started heading up a nearby mountain, away from the main ruins. They all had some worksheets to fill out, though it seemed like the teachers were just trying to keep the kids busy so they wouldn't get into too many shenanigans. Thankfully, it wasn't a full-scale exchange between the two kingdoms. Having more than a few Nefarians around ran the risk that they might pull a scheme on the locals and create a diplomatic incident, which was something that happened commonly on Nefarian field trips. Usually, it was resolved without war, which was the only reason these trips were still allowed to happen, though they tended to be limited to small groups.

There were some Jovialese students following Candelabra

and her friends, though everyone in the two groups was still too shy to mingle. If Shmebecca had been around, she might have helped merge everyone together, but apparently, she was not allowed to go on field trips to the mountain during school hours anymore due to "a tendency to get distracted," as she'd put it to Candelabra and Bobert the night before. The words had been accompanied by a hearty eye roll.

Candelabra was lost in thought when she felt the ground shaking. She wasn't even sure how long it had been going on when she snapped out of her reverie, because her friends were already shouting and trying to hang on for dear life. Bobert, who had been sketching some rock formations in the distance, had run to a nearby tree for safety. Except that, not having any prior experience with earthquakes, he hadn't thought about how stuff might fall from above when things were violently shaking. So now he was trying to both hang on to the tree trunk and protect his head from the acorns and branches raining down on him.

"What do we do?" Stanbert shouted.

"What's happening?" Candelabra said, even though she realized as soon as she'd asked.

They'd been told about earthquakes, of course, and what to do in case one occurred during their field trip. But being prepared for a natural disaster in theory doesn't really matter in the moment when you're experiencing it for the first time.

THE GREATEST HEIST IN JOVIALA

The earth was doing something Candelabra had never felt before, and maybe that, more than anything, was what scared her. Not even the notion that someone was doing this on purpose to harm others would have scared her more.

The noise wasn't helping at all. It sounded like all the rocks beneath the earth's surface were being torn apart. Or like the mountain they were on was trying to rip away from the ground to go elsewhere. And it was terrifying to feel the power being unleashed everywhere all at once, to not know what it would do to the mountain, what it would do to her. She knew just how quickly everything could be taken from her.

She found herself mimicking Stanbert's half-squatting pose, hands gripping the tufts of wild grass.

And then, just as suddenly as it had begun, the shaking stopped.

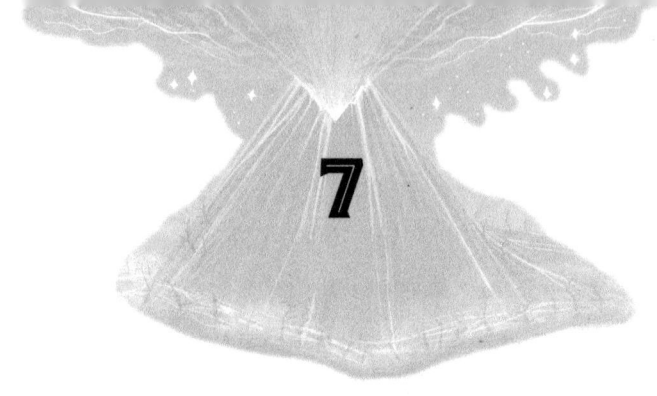

7

ONCE THE DANGER SEEMED TO BE OVER, BOBERT AND HIS friends shared a nervous look before breaking out in laughter.

"That was wild!" Stanbert cackled, his voice giving away the little bit of terror that Bobert himself was still feeling too.

"I can't believe they just live with those all the time," Jennizabeth mumbled.

"Should we go over to the group and tell them we're okay?" Bobert asked. They'd gotten a bit separated from the other kids, some of whom were running around playing tag at the bottom of the hill as if nothing had happened. He had a giddy feeling in his stomach, like he'd just survived something intensely dangerous, like he was lucky to be alive. He knew it was silly to feel that way, but he hadn't had that experience before, and even though it was scary, it was a little exciting, too.

"We already went all this way—if we turn around now, we're not gonna see what's up this hill," Candelabra said.

The group argued for a little while about what to do, and

though Bobert felt it was best to check in with the adults, arguments tended to tire him out, so he let the others figure out what was best. He meandered in the field they were in, looking for rocks that he could sketch for Mr. Gigglebutt's assignment.

Then he heard a rumbling that got his heart racing, making him think that another earthquake was coming. He braced himself against a nearby tree again, apparently not having learned his lesson about falling branches.

Thankfully, it seemed like the noise was just a noise. *Un*thankfully, Bobert's friends had seen him run to the tree.

"What are you doing?" Stanbert asked, raising an eyebrow. And Stanbert could raise an eyebrow higher than anyone Bobert had ever met.

He cleared his throat and let go of the tree. "Did you all hear something?"

The rumbling grew louder, as if to make sure it was heard; then it was punctuated with a boom. The kids shared a look and then moved toward the sound. "I don't know why we always have to be moving *toward* sounds," Stanbert said, and they all shushed him.

Cutting across the trees and through some brush, they came upon the same field where Shmebecca had discovered the construction project. Bobert and Candelabra guessed as much, and they filled their friends in on what Shmebecca had told them the night before.

"I know I'm going to regret asking this," Jennizabeth said, "but how are we supposed to help? We're only here for a few days."

"I don't know," Candelabra answered. "But we should get closer and see what we can find out. Maybe there's a crucial piece of equipment we can sabotage and solve the whole thing in two seconds."

Unlike Shmebecca, they didn't know that marching through the project to go talk to whoever was in charge was an option. They probably could have asked any one of the workers directly if there was a crucial piece of equipment that would ruin it all. The Jovialese construction crew would have gladly pointed at it and said, "It sure would be terrible if that thingamajig went missing!"

But these were Nefarian children, who knew that if you were scheming about something or other, no matter if it was for good and not evil, you had to sneak around. They split up into groups of two, since sneaking around as a group of four was hard, even for the sneakiest Nefarians.

Bobert paired up with Jennizabeth, and they maneuvered their way from tree to tree along the outskirts of the construction site, trying to find some rolled-up schematics or something. Bobert wasn't entirely sure what they were looking for, if he was being honest.

THE GREATEST HEIST IN JOVIALA

"Those people look important," Jennizabeth whispered. She was pointing at a short man wearing a cape and a tall, thin woman with cat-eye glasses and a gold brooch on her lapel. "Let's get close and try to eavesdrop."

They scurried from one tree to the next. Just beyond the tree line, Bobert could see Stanbert and Candelabra crawling on their bellies in some tall grass, with no clear destination. But they were sneaking really well, so when he made eye contact with Candelabra, he gave her a thumbs-up. It was comforting, in a way, to be doing something that reminded him of home. It was nice to have that among all the new things in Joviala.

When they got close to the people Jennizabeth had spotted, they tiptoed to the closest tree, then rolled on the ground to hide behind a boulder. Thankfully, they were both very good rollers, having had plenty of practice on the hill outside of school in Nefaria. *Un*thankfully, the important-looking man and woman were just talking about a salad they had had for lunch. (Bobert made a note to himself to look up the word "thankfully" in the thesaurus to find antonyms.)

"I think that was the best salad I've ever eaten!" the man exclaimed. "And I'm a big salad guy. You know how I like my salads."

"I do know, Shmelson!" The woman laughed.

Did everyone in Joviala speak solely in exclamation marks?

A few moments later the two were joined by a woman with an elaborate hairdo made to look like an eagle was perched on her head and eating a snake (which was reading a book).

"Another one?" the eagle-hair lady asked.

"Yes," the lady with the brooch responded, not missing a beat. "Another salad—isn't Shmelson obsessed?"

"I meant the earthquake!"

"Well, yes," Shmelson grumbled. "That was always part of the expectation, as I understand it. Moving the mountain will create further Natural Inconveniences, but nothing that should cause us any undue concern. As you know, Mr. Eyebrows has confirmed that the project was stamped by the board as being Totally Fine."

"Of course, of course. And the lasagnanite we're going to mine from this operation alone makes it all worth it—"

"Plus all the riches and fun we'll get from the adventure park!" the brooch woman said, dancing in place as she said it.

"Yes, the fun and riches will be appreciated," Eagle-Hair Lady said, adding her own little dance with way too much arm movement. "I know it all carries the distinction of being Totally Fine and Profitable, so everything will be great. I just wish the extra earthquakes and possible volcanic eruptions weren't part of the deal. They really put a damper on my morning. I spilled a little of my coffee today!" she exclaimed, and all three of them broke into extended laughter.

Still crouching behind the boulder, Bobert and Jennizabeth shared a look. "That doesn't sound good," Jennizabeth said. Bobert shook his head and peeked around the side of the boulder again.

"It's not something we should worry about, is it?" Eagle-Hair asked, as if she'd heard Jennizabeth.

"Oh, just in the way we worry about most Natural Inconveniences," Brooch responded, literally waving the worry away. "Sure, they might ramp up progressively as the project goes on, culminating in some sort of unpredictable large-scale event with unanticipated consequences." She said this casually, as if she were reading a list of procedures for a Council of Elders meeting. "But Mr. Eyebrows approved everything, so even if those things do happen, the joy portion of the equation has all been properly balanced, I'm sure." She reached over and put a hand on Eagle-Hair's forearm. "You're such a worrier!" And then the trio laughed again, craning their necks all the way back so their laughter was directed up to the sky. It was a laugh Nefarians were very used to hearing.

After learning what they had learned, it was hard to explore the grounds and just take notes about the ruins and rocks. Bobert couldn't help but feel like the unpredictable large-scale event the woman had talked about was going to happen at any moment. He wanted to run to town and warn everyone about the dangers this construction crew was knowingly subjecting them to.

But, again, the children of Nefaria (most of them, anyway) were used to the world being a certain way, and, for better or for worse, so were their teachers. They couldn't overreact to every bit of bad news. It would be exhausting!

That being said, Bobert wasn't surprised when Candelabra walked up to Mr. Gigglebutt and announced that there was an evil scheme in the works and that they all had a responsibility to stop it. In Nefaria, protocol dictated that the first time someone announced there was an evil scheme afoot, you had to ignore them and probably roll your eyes. The second time, you would probably roll your eyes again, but then, depending on your position of power, you had to report the potential scheme to a local sniffer-outer. Then you'd have to file paperwork with the Council of Elders, after which there would be no fewer than eight follow-up hearings to make sure everything had been properly investigated and no evil was afoot.

These were measures that had been put in place in Nefaria a long time ago out of necessity. They weren't perfect, but they worked well enough.

Unfortunately, they only applied to Nefaria. To make matters worse, Candelabra had a reputation around school for being eager to blow the whistle on evil schemes. Granted, she'd been right last time, and had helped save Bobert. But Mr. Gigglebutt still chuckled when she unleashed her warning, thinking she was making some sort of joke.

Mr. Gigglebutt offered a smile to the Jovialese teachers, but his cheeks reddened as he leaned over to get eye to eye with her. "Listen, Candy, we all admire your vigilance. But this isn't Nefaria. It's okay to let go a little here."

"Does an 'unpredictable large-scale event with unintended consequences' sound like something we can all just relax about?" she huffed.

That was when Imogene Petunias stepped in to lead Candelabra away somewhere quieter. Bobert watched as Candelabra gestured, snippets of what she was saying carrying over on the breeze. ". . . just 'cause it's . . . We have to try! . . . Explosions! She used that word!"

He had seen Candelabra's passion for thwarting evil schemes from afar before they were really friends. There was the time a sixth grader had tried to use mind control to rig the class elections, but Candelabra had noticed a thought that wasn't like her and gone straight to the school's evil-scheme liaison. Then, of course, there was the fact that she had been the only one to come looking for him, the only one who'd believed an evil scheme was afoot, even though she couldn't remember him at the time (that had been part of the curse).

It was comforting in a way. Amid the excitement of the exchange trip, Bobert had felt a little afraid that things might change. That the new normal he'd been enjoying ever since they'd escaped the castle could disappear in Joviala, or when they got back home. But Candelabra was still the same person he knew. He still had all these friends. Nothing was going to change just because they were having a little adventure. Other kids were glancing over now, ignoring Mr. Gigglebutt's attempts to quiz them about what they had learned throughout the day.

When Candelabra eventually came back to the group, the scowl on her face told Bobert everything he needed to know. "Miss Petunias doesn't want to make a big deal of it, since we don't actually know what's happening and evil's not a part of the culture here or whatever," Candelabra said to Bobert and the others.

"So what do we do now?" Jennizabeth asked.

"We go home immediately, far away from mountains that can explode," Stanbert said.

"Or we talk to someone local who is willing to act," Bobert jumped in.

Stanbert glanced over at the cratered peak of Mount Saint Helenhunt. "I don't know exactly how volcanoes work, so I vote we get as far away from that thing as possible."

Bobert rolled his eyes at Stanbert, who said stuff like that all the time even though he didn't mean it. "Shmebecca's gonna be at the lunch they're having for us," he said. "We'll tell her what we learned and figure out a plan."

Bobert looked over at Candelabra, who had pulled her wizard tablet from her backpack and was typing something in. "What are you looking at?"

"Lasagnanite? I thought they couldn't find that anymore," Candelabra said. "You overheard that woman saying something about it, right?"

Bobert paid the most attention in geology, but he didn't remember learning about a rock called lasagnanite. He shrugged along with everyone else, and was about to ask Candelabra why it mattered when the adults called out that it was time to hop back on their bicycles to head to lunch.

The whole ride back, Bobert couldn't help but hope that this was all just some big misunderstanding. That he'd be able to enjoy traveling for the first time, and that Shmebecca was overreacting. This was Joviala, after all. Chances were everything would be fine.

Shmebecca's school had set up a party of sorts on the field. There were a handful of local food stands, two bands (which seemed to be competing, each one playing its music louder and louder, trying to drown out the other band), a lot of flaming balloons, and what seemed to be a petting zoo, although that could have just been a bunch of wild animals huddled together in a corner of the field—Bobert wasn't too sure.

There was also a stage set up, above which hung a large banner that read WELCOME NEFARIANS TO THE HAPPIEST KINGDOM AROUND! A woman stood at the podium at center stage, quietly mouthing words she was reading off a note card.

The school itself was a handful of separate squat buildings surrounding the field, and now Bobert saw Shmebecca burst out of one of them and come running toward him and Candelabra, a tote bag full of books bouncing at her side. She arrived a little out of breath but seemed eager to ask them how the day had gone. "Did you find anything out? Did you see the construction crew?"

Candelabra bit her bottom lip and pretended to get distracted by the bands playing their saxophones aggressively at each other. Bobert could see the pain on her face at the idea of delivering bad news to Shmebecca, so he jumped in and told her what they'd learned.

Bobert was expecting her face to fall, if not flat-out cry again, but Shmebecca took it well. Maybe it was because of how public a setting they were in, or maybe it was hard to cry to the background sounds of dueling saxophones. Or maybe it was just that Shmebecca had cried all the tears she'd needed to the night before, and now was the time to fight back.

"Okay," she said, nodding. She peered around the field, which was filling up with her schoolmates, who were looking curiously over at the Nefarian kids. "First . . . have you had fried doughy thingies?" Her jaw was set, as if she were asking them an extremely important question.

Bobert shook his head.

"Okay, we're gonna get you some fried doughy thingies, because they're delightful, and it's a travesty that you haven't had any yet. Then we're gonna call for a town hall."

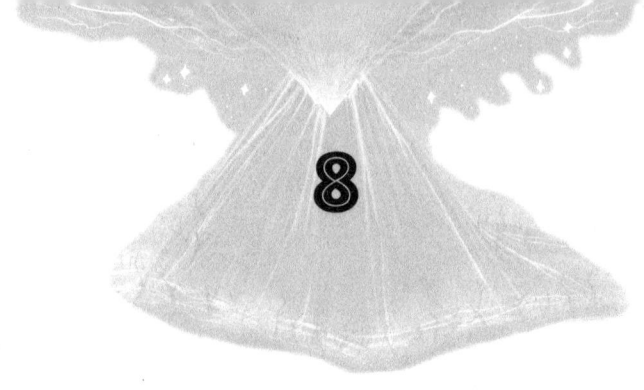

TOWN HALLS IN JOVIALA WERE NOT LIKE THEY WERE IN Nefaria. There was a lot less yelling; fewer parents worried about their children getting stuck in quicksand; and fewer accusations of corruption, evil schemes, or general ne'er-do-welling. There were much better snacks, and generally a more pleasant vibe. Jovialese town halls were more like block parties than places to air out civic grievances.

It was not all that different from the welcome party Shmebecca's school had thrown for the Nefarian visitors, just with more adults around and fewer animals (though there were still a few).

Shmebecca had explained to Bobert and Candelabra that every citizen in Joviala, regardless of their age, had the right to call for a town hall at any time. Usually, people did it because it was their birthday and they wanted the excuse to have people gather in their honor, or because they were feeling a little lonelier than usual and needed a catered pick-me-up. Occasionally town halls were used for their intended purpose: to call attention to something that needed fixing, or because someone needed to complain and the people close to them were sick of hearing about it, so they brought the complainer to a wider audience.

After the welcome party, Shmebecca had gone to the Office of Townly Matters and rung the town-hall request bell, which automatically scheduled one for that evening. They made her fill out some paperwork about how long she wanted the floor for and for what general purpose. There was another form to request any snack (she had to admit she got some pleasure out of writing down her favorite snack: fish doughnuts). When she was done, she had just enough time to go home, write a rough draft of what she wanted to say, tell her parents about the town hall, and then head back to the public amphitheater where all important civic gatherings were held.

Shmary and Shmarcos had been very excited, not just because the Nefarian kids and their chaperones would get to experience the fun, but because it was the first time Shmebecca would be speaking at a town hall. They hadn't seemed too concerned by the fact that the Fun Corporation was at the heart of the matter again. "Oh, those people have equipment lying about everywhere," her dad had said with a laugh. "A coincidence like this was bound to happen eventually."

That didn't exactly make Shmebecca feel better.

Now she stood off to the side of the stage, making corrections to the speech she'd prepared. She looked out at the audience and rolled her eyes while she waved at her parents, who were sitting in the front row munching on popcorn with huge grins on their faces. Even the twins beamed at her, and she couldn't help but smile back at them. Bobert and Candelabra were sitting quietly beside the twins, looking around the amphitheater, taking in the sights.

Just as she turned back to her note cards, something clicked for her. A face in the crowd that she just now realized she recognized. Looking up, she tried to find the man again, but more and more people were streaming in, making it hard to spot him. She was about to chalk it up to her imagination, when a group of snail-people who had been talking in the aisle moved out of the way, and she saw him again: Mr. Eyebrows.

Her heart began pounding in her chest, and she tightened her grip on her note cards. She hadn't expected him to be there. Rather than tear the papers up and throw them at him like she wanted to do, Shmebecca focused on the words she'd written, using her pencil to make a few last-second additions.

She couldn't afford for her speech to land softly. She needed the adults of Joviala to understand that they couldn't just move a mountain with no consequences. Especially not *her* mountain. Did she know exactly what those consequences would be? No, not entirely. But that was the point. They needed to halt

THE GREATEST HEIST IN JOVIALA

the construction project until some volcanologists could determine the dangers, at the very least.

This was a mountain that saved lives. Hers, of course. But in the years since the mountain had saved her from the Fun Corporation's negligence, she'd spent a lot of time there and learned how its nutrient-rich soil helped grow a lot of the food that fed not just Joviala's people, but also its animals and half-people-half-animal hybrid beings. And all the creatures in other kingdoms that ate Jovialese food too. The mountain also helped shield her town from storms that came in from the west. On top of that, the various minerals found within Mount Saint Helenhunt were used for a whole slew of things, including healing potions and refrigeration rocks that helped prolong food shelf life. The very mud that Shmebecca had almost drowned in was used to help older people's backs feel better. That one didn't really save any lives, but it made it so that you didn't have to hear those older people make exaggerated noises every time they sat on or got up from a couch.

Trying not to look over at either her parents or Mr. Eyebrows, Shmebecca quietly practiced reading her speech out loud. Her mouth went dry when her eyes flitted away from the note cards to see that the amphitheater was almost completely full. (It seemed that word had spread about the fish doughnuts.) The biggest crowd she'd ever spoken to was her class when giving a presentation, and even that had been nerve-racking.

Mayor Shmayor made her way to the podium, the clack of her boots reverberating throughout the amphitheater, quieting the audience. Shmebecca would have preferred if the crowd kept talking for another five to sixty minutes.

Mayor Shmayor smiled from center stage. Even though the Jovialese were a very smiley people, Mayor Shmayor was one of the smiliest. And, it was widely agreed upon, she had one of the best smiles around. Bright-eyed and with the exact right teeth-to-lips ratio, her smile made people feel like everything was going to be okay.

"Good evening, everyone," she began, speaking into the microphone (which was really just a magically enhanced can of beans). "It is a joy to be here with you." There were some cheers and clapping from the audience, as usual.

Shmebecca tried to keep her mind on her note cards and her speech. She was vaguely aware of the mayor giving her usual updates on traffic, weather, and recent magical accomplishments, as well as the crowd's oohs, aahs, and other reactions.

Then the mayor was saying Shmebecca's name, and one of the town-hall ushers placed a gentle hand on her back to guide her toward the stage. Polite applause accompanied her walk to the podium, along with slightly restrained cheering from her parents. The supportive noise allowed her to think that maybe, despite her nervousness, what she'd written was as good as she felt it was. That she'd be able to speak loudly and clearly like her public-speaking teacher had taught her in class. She'd make such good eye contact around the room that people would whisper to each other, "Wow, are you seeing this eye contact?" And they wouldn't even be able to look away as they whispered. Maybe she'd have such good eye contact that she'd be able to see her fellow Jovialese citizens start to care.

With this image in mind, she gave the traditional greeting. "It is a joy to be here with you," she said, as loudly as she could manage. It was a little shocking to hear how her voice carried in the acoustics of the amphitheater. Maybe that would help her deliver her message, and something would immediately be done. Maybe that was how close she was to waking up from this nightmare.

She began to read, imagining her lungs filling up, her voice growing louder. She let the thought of rescuing her mountain straighten her spine, and she thought she even delivered a line with the kind of fiery passion that always marked great speeches. "This mountain is my favorite mountain and a very good mountain and moving it would be not good and maybe even really bad so we shouldn't move it or let anyone else move it for any reason but especially not to build a road or anything else. Like, can't they build around the mountain or maybe even a tunnel, although that's a bad idea too. The mountain is so important to the ecosystem and also to life. To my life and to yours."

She took a breath and risked looking up at the crowd. She hoped to catch at least one person in the audience looking moved to action. They didn't have to be crying, but they probably would be. Night had arrived, though, and the overhead lights had just been flicked on by the amphitheater's light wizard, the glare making it hard to observe the crowd. But that just made it easier to imagine them out there, speechless and moved by her passion. Shmebecca kept reading, feeling more and more confident with each line.

"My friends—well, not really friends, they're just visiting from Nefaria, but I think they're friendly—they overheard people at the construction site saying that the project was going to cause a lot of damage. I didn't actually write down the term for some reason, or I had it in one of these note cards; somehow they're all out of order now. The important part is that the people trying to move the mountain know that something bad could happen, but they don't care!" She smacked her fist down on the podium for effect.

By the time she finished, she was fully expecting a roar of applause to punctuate her last line. Instead she heard someone clear their throat, a glass getting knocked over and breaking, and then some more polite clapping, followed by her mom loudly calling out: "You did great, honey!"

Oh god. She had not done great, had she?

Before she knew it, the town-hall usher was leading her

back off the stage, and the mayor was clacking her way to the podium again. Shmebecca felt like she needed to simultaneously pause time, throw up, cry, cheer, and maybe interview every single person in attendance to ask what had just happened. She almost felt like she was stuck in the hot mud springs again, unable to catch her breath or even swim to safety.

It was all made so much worse, though, when Mayor Shmayor introduced their next speaker. "Please join me in welcoming Mr. Eyebrows, here from the Fun Corporation, with a rebuttal to the um . . . speech . . . we just heard."

Now Shmebecca really felt like throwing up. She walked in a daze to the available seat between her parents and Candelabra, hoping that her dad's popcorn bucket was empty in case she ended up spewing like a volcano. They were going to give the Fun Corporation a chance to make up excuses again? To convince everyone that what they were doing was fine?

"Thank you for that warm welcome, Mayor Shmayor!" Mr. Eyebrows said, marching up to the stage with a big, stupid smile on his face like he wasn't threatening to destroy everything precious to Shmebecca. "And thank you, Shmebecca, for taking the time to share that angry, muttering performance-art piece. I very much support young people speaking up for what they believe in, and to do it in really weird and ineffective ways!" He made a show of clapping in her direction, and a few others in the crowd clapped along. Shmebecca felt her cheeks flush. She wondered if anyone would stop her if she ran back to the stage to tackle him.

She was hit by flashbacks to being eight years old, those terrifying moments facedown in the mud, sure that her silly decision to follow the gentleman bug would end up being her premature doom. Afterward, just happy she was alive, she'd have an icky feeling whenever she heard of the Fun Corporation. But it had clearly been an accident, even if it was an avoidable one. And once they'd paid a fine and apologized, there was nothing much for Shmebecca's family to do about it.

"I signed up to speak when I knew the subject matter of the instigating town-hall request, because I wanted to make sure both sides of the story were represented," Mr. Eyebrows said, smiling, which sent shivers down Shmebecca's spine. "I'd like everyone to rest assured that our project has a Totally Fine certification and went through all the proper channels to ensure everything is as safe as possible. Our internal team conducted a survey and found that the chances of increased Natural Inconveniences, while possible, are negligible. Especially when we consider the benefits of this project."

He looked to the side of the stage and made a beckoning motion with his hand. A woman with an elaborate hairdo in the shape of what appeared to be a puppy juggling six knives carried an incredibly large easel awkwardly toward him. It was covered by a piece of beige fabric that kept sliding off and tripping her. Mr. Eyebrows did nothing to help her, Shmebecca couldn't help but notice. After a couple of stumbles, she placed it beside Mr. Eyebrows, smoothed out her dress, and then walked offstage.

"Since there hasn't been a formal announcement, I thought I'd take advantage of this town hall to fill you in on all the wonderful things this project will provide. So"—he looked pointedly at Shmebecca—"thank you, little one, for giving me this opportunity."

With a flourish, he unveiled the easel. The words WELCOME TO ADVENTURE LAND were written in bold letters above a scene depicting water slides, roller coasters, and an illustrated child happily lapping up some ice cream while riding a dragon. Nowhere on the poster could Shmebecca see Mount Saint Helenhunt. The crowd behind her started murmuring excitedly. When she turned to look over her shoulder, she could see people half standing to get a better look, big smiles on their faces.

Mr. Eyebrows went on to list all the rides and features the park would have, while Shmebecca sat there alternating between bouts of nausea and fuming with rage. Her dad put a hand on her shoulder and leaned in to whisper that it would all be okay, but it was hard to feel like that could be possible.

All Shmebecca could think about was when her parents had found her beside the hot mud spring, how they'd held her close, crying happy tears that she was okay. When she'd explained what had happened, her dad had knelt down and kissed the ground, thanking the mountain for saving her. Her mom had gone over to the water pump and kicked it angrily. The following weeks had been busy with her parents trying to get answers as to how the Fun Corporation's carelessness had almost led to tragedy.

Now here the Fun Corporation was again, not just being careless accidentally, but purposefully, it seemed. And they weren't just going to move a mountain a little bit for a road. They were going to get rid of it entirely. "Why is an amusement park more important than the mountain?" Shmebecca grumbled.

"Why is everyone just believing what he says? This guy is clearly a schemer," Candelabra said beside her. Shmebecca gave her a half-hearted smile, thankful for the support in this roomful of people who seemed to be swallowing Mr. Eyebrows's presentation.

"Some of you may be wondering why an amusement park is more important than a mountain," Mr. Eyebrows said, and Shmebecca huffed again. He grabbed the easel and moved the poster on it to reveal a second one. It was divided down the middle. On the left there was a drawing of Shmebecca's mountain with the words NO FUN written over it. On the right was a depiction of the amusement park with a lot of drawings of

THE GREATEST HEIST IN JOVIALA

children smiling Mr. Eyebrows's same unnatural smile. That side of the board was labeled with a huge FUN!

"The short answer, and the most important one . . ." He pointed at the word with his index finger, beaming at the audience, his teeth so bright they almost hurt Shmebecca's eyes. "We at the Fun Corporation deeply believe that the more fun there is to be had in a town or a kingdom, the better off that kingdom is."

The audience responded with applause, and Shmebecca folded her arms across her chest.

"That's not all, though!" Mr. Eyebrows flipped to one last poster. This one was a chart with a line graph on it, the arrow moving in a perfect diagonal up to the right. The X axis was labeled LASAGNANITE, while the Y axis read RICHES FOR JOVIALA. Beside her, Candelabra gasped. Shmebecca turned to make sure she was okay, but Candelabra just stared ahead and began chewing her nails as Mr. Eyebrows continued. "Since we will have to excavate some land for the road leading to the park, and for the park itself, we've been running some tests on the ground in the area. Again, this is to make sure it's all safe and sound. We care about this town and the kingdom as much as anyone, after all! That is why we're working so hard to provide you with all this fun!"

He chuckled like he'd just told a joke, almost baring his teeth as he did. There was something about him that made

Shmebecca deeply uncomfortable, especially because no one else seemed to sense that there was something wrong with this whole situation. Sometimes it felt like everyone in Joviala wanted to pretend nothing bad ever happened there.

"As you see here in this chart, we've discovered large pockets of lasagnanite in the mountain. We will simply relocate Mount Saint Helenhunt a few dozen . . . hundred . . . feet. Now, as you all know, land can't be torn apart simply for its resources, unless they're discovered during the construction of a pre-approved project. So it's a matter of good luck that all this lasagnanite was discovered at all! We found it not too long ago during routine cleanings of the hot mud springs along the mountain. Not only is it going to be a valuable trading asset with other kingdoms, enriching Joviala for years to come, but does anyone here know the practical uses for this incredible mineral?"

There were a few shouted responses from the crowd, including the mayor, who said, "Lasagna!"

Shmebecca's leg started jittering beyond control, and she noticed that Candelabra's leg was also bouncing up and down. Bobert was looking at both of them, and he mouthed, *Are you okay?* Shmebecca could only shrug and shake her head no.

"That's right," Mr. Eyebrows laughed. "Lasagnanite is used in the production of the famous casserole dishes used to bake our Jovialese delicacy: lasagna. For those children visiting from Nefaria, that's a baked recipe made of pasta, tomato sauce, cheese, and snakes! Very delicious! But there are a few other uses of this wonderful mineral: it's crucial in construction, has proven to have healing properties when turned into soap, and for centuries it has been a key ingredient in witches' potions and pomades to help break curses. Isn't that wonderful?"

Shmebecca thought she heard Candelabra take in a sharp breath again, but the sound was lost among the cheers from the crowd. Happy, excited cheers agreeing with the conniving man who was going to steal her mountain. Who was convincing Joviala that the mountain was a worthy price to pay for a little enjoyment and some money. No one was jeering at him; no one was screaming out objections.

She thought about going up there herself and shouting "Are you serious?" at the crowd for the next hour, or maybe chaining herself to the podium until volcanologists were called in to advise on the project, until *someone* was called to make sure no one would get hurt. That her mountain wouldn't get hurt, her precious mountain and its wildlife, its rocks big and small, its lifesaving burps. But she was too stunned to move. And she didn't actually have any chains with her.

Some people started chanting, "Move that mountain!" And Mr. Eyebrows clapped along to the rhythm of their chanting, every now and then making eye contact with Shmebecca and giving her a thumbs-up.

Shmebecca watched in quiet horror. Instead of helping rescue her mountain, the town hall that she had called to interrupt the construction project turned into a celebration of it.

9

SHMEBENEZER EYEBROWS BELIEVED IN FUN. IN HIS OPINION, there was nothing more important in the world. It was why he had started his company, and why he searched all over Joviala (and perhaps some other kingdoms) in search of how to find more fun. Fun he could pump out of the very ground, not just for himself, but to share with the people around him.

He had been happy with how the town hall had gone, for the most part. That red-cheeked girl with the hair tie that was hanging on for dear life had not seemed to be having fun. Not even after he had explained all the wonderful things the Fun Corporation was going to do with that useless bit of land.

As he settled in for the evening with a glass of spider wine and all the paperwork he had filed with the Jovialese government, he wondered if the girl was maybe not from Joviala at all. He knew people from other kingdoms that she reminded him of, and he was curious to know if she was really Jovialese.

For someone from this joyful kingdom, she sure seemed to focus on not-fun things.

As he reviewed the plan for the upcoming days, he took note of the girl who had spoken: Shmebecca Ferguson. The name rang a bell for some reason, and he had the feeling that it would be wise to keep an eye on her. She might need some convincing that everything he was doing was for the good of Joviala.

But he doubted that he would have to worry about her much. Joviala was a land that embraced fun. It embraced people who sought out fun, like him. No matter what a person's background was, this land was welcoming to people like him: people who knew joy and how to spread it.

10

Candelabra lay awake most of the night, telling herself that it was because of the new surroundings. This was only her second night in a strange bed, in a strange land, and the noises coming through the twins' cracked open bedroom window weren't the ones she was used to. There were no braying goats hunting for their prey, no singing mountain spiders in the distance. There was just Bobert's soft snoring from the other bed, the gentle rustling of leaves in the breeze, and her thoughts.

What Mr. Eyebrows had said kept repeating itself in her mind, even though she tried to steer her thoughts toward sleep. She knew that there weren't supposed to be evil schemes here, but there was something about that man that felt schemey, if not downright evil. Maybe she just thought that because she was from Nefaria, or because of her personal history. Either way, she found it hard to trust what he'd said.

Surprisingly, though, the thought of an evil scheme happening in Joviala wasn't what was keeping her awake. Something else had been turning over and over in her mind ever since the town hall ended. It was mostly just that word, "lasagnanite," repeating itself like a nagging classmate whispering in her ear.

In the morning, thankful that she'd gotten any sleep at all, Candelabra rolled out of bed to the sound of voices in the other room. Everyone had woken up before her, it seemed (she knew one of the twins had, because he'd screamed for twenty minutes). In the kitchen she found Shmarcos making pancakes at the stove, and one of the twins was on a little stepstool beside him, holding a spatula.

Shmebecca, Bobert, Shmary, and the other twin were at the table, picking at a bowl of fresh fruit. For a moment, everything that had kept Candelabra awake was forgotten. She realized how long it had been since she'd woken up to a full house, to the smell of breakfast and the sound of people talking. Okay, it had only been yesterday. But before that, it had been two years. Practically an eternity for a twelve-year-old. Her stomach fluttered with joy, especially when they all noticed her presence and offered smiling good-mornings.

She took a seat next to Bobert and peered into the fruit bowl, which held all sorts of berries she wasn't familiar with.

THE GREATEST HEIST IN JOVIALA

Using the slotted spoon, she served herself a sample, and tuned into the conversation.

"I know it's frustrating, honey," Shmary was saying. "But sometimes we have to trust that the people in charge are doing their best."

"But I don't trust them!" Shmebecca huffed. "We need to do something. I don't understand why you're not upset. At least help me brainstorm."

Shmary sighed and leaned over to plant a kiss on her daughter's head. Shmebecca leaned back in her chair and crossed her arms over her chest.

Shmary smiled at Candelabra and Bobert. "Anyway! What do they have planned for you all today?"

Bobert started running through the schedule, which started with sitting in on a couple of classes to experience what school in Joviala was like, followed by rafting and other water activities in the natural springs outside town (not the muddy ones). Candelabra had forgotten about the plans, and hearing about them filled her with glee, especially once she tasted one of the orange berries on her plate. It was tart and sweet and a little spicy, too, like nothing she'd ever tasted before. It reminded her about the possibility of change. Of new, exciting things entering her life, and maybe bad things leaving.

Shborris and Shmorris giggled about something, and a

butterfly fluttered in through the open window and landed on her nose. Candelabra went cross-eyed watching it, at which point the butterfly smiled, revealing two rows of perfectly white humanoid teeth. In Nefaria it would have been a terrifying sight, but here, somehow, it was adorable. Joviala was an incredible place.

Then she noticed Shmebecca pushing the fruit around on her plate. It reminded her of her sleepless night and of lasagnanite, of Sandraliere back home, of falling prey to evil schemes. She reached over and squeezed Shmebecca's shoulder, offering what she hoped was a reassuring smile when their eyes met. She wanted to be supportive, but maybe after this delightful morning was over. Shmebecca returned the smile, and maybe she could read Candelabra's thoughts, because she didn't say anything either, saving it until they were walking to her school.

They were strolling alongside a picturesque creek that ran right from Shmebecca's backyard to the campus, which was a perfectly flat and pleasant fifteen-minute walk away. Back home, Candelabra had to walk up a hill, then down, then back up to get to school, and it never took less than forty minutes.

"So, it looks like the adults around here are all happy to let some weirdo with a construction company just destroy a million-year-old mountain, but I'm not. I have an idea, and I'll probably need help," Shmebecca said, running her fingertips

THE GREATEST HEIST IN JOVIALA

along some tall grass and not looking up at either Candelabra or Bobert. "If you don't want to help, that's okay. Just don't tell anyone that I said anything."

Candelabra took a deep breath, quieting the little nagging voice in her head that just wanted to enjoy this kingdom and its lack of evil schemes. The voice that told her she had her own problems to worry about. She didn't know where this voice had come from, but it didn't sound entirely like her own. "What's your idea?"

The briefest smile flashed across Shmebecca's face; then she furrowed her brow again, like she was trying to solve a math problem. "I still have a few things to figure out. Talk to your friends and see if they can help. I'll do the same. We're gonna need as many people as we can get."

The school came into view now, and Candelabra could see all the Jovialese students arriving. Some were being walked by their families, some walked alongside a friend or two, and some arrived on the backs of rat-birds, which kissed them on the forehead at the entrance to the school and then took off into the sky.

"What do you want us to do?" Bobert asked Shmebecca.

"We should have some time before the bonfire they're holding for you all tonight. How long are you here for?"

"Four more days," Bobert answered. "We leave on Flormsday."

Shmebecca took a deep breath and nodded. "Okay. We'll meet at those picnic tables in front of the school. I'll have the plan ready by then."

An undercurrent of anxiety stuck with Candelabra the rest of the day. She was placed in Shmebecca's math class with Mr. Shmigglebutt (no relation to Mr. Gigglebutt) for the morning. She was fascinated by how chipper the redheaded teacher was, how his word problems never used some uncomfortable scenario where the students had to figure out how many vampires they had to kill in order to break the exponential spread of vampirism in the population. Throughout the morning Candelabra watched Shmebecca, who was scribbling in her notebook, although it didn't seem like she was doing any math.

After that they were given a tour of the school, and in the library Candelabra had the urge to sneak into the science aisles to look up lasagnanite, but before she had a chance, they were whisked away to the natural springs for a day in the sun.

Candelabra had never seen water so clear and warm. There was a gently flowing, deep river where the kids could float along on inflatable rafts, or dive down with snorkels to look

THE GREATEST HEIST IN JOVIALA

at the colorful fish, eels, and crabs that scurried this way and that. There were even a couple of waterslides built along the side of a waterfall.

While they were having lunch at the snack bar (it was curious to see that the corn dog was popular both in Joviala and Nefaria, although in Nefaria it was a bunch of corn shaped to resemble a dog, and here it was a hot dog shaped to look like an ear of corn), Candelabra and the rest of the Nefarians were confused when it appeared to start snowing. It was only when the flakes started landing on them and smearing streaks of black and gray on their swim-wrinkled skin that they realized it wasn't snow at all, but ash.

"Nope!" Stanbert said, gathering his lunch and running toward the stone locker-room building.

Jennizabeth covered her head with her towel and squinted up at the sky. Even though it was initially scary, Candelabra found it to be kind of beautiful, those little black flakes dancing in the blue sky. One landed on Bobert's nose, and when he tried to wipe it away it smeared and turned his nose dark, reminding her of that brief time when he'd been a sloth.

Then Miss Petunias came around to let them know that it was a normal eruption from a nearby active volcano, Xocoataptatlataptalt, and that the ash probably had restorative properties for their skin, whatever that meant. Miss Petunias often said things they didn't entirely understand. If they were being honest, there was a lot about Miss Petunias they didn't understand.

Other than that, it was a delightful day all around. Even the volcanic eruption was new and exciting. It made her hungry to explore other lands, since she had never been to a part of the world that was quite like this one, and it made her wonder what else was out there. What else could she see if Sandraliere weren't shackled to that painting above the mantelpiece?

By the time they left the natural baths and arrived back at Shmebecca's school, Candelabra had almost forgotten about meeting up with her for the plan. But then Bobert led them away from the hubbub of the crowd and filled Stanbert and Jennizabeth in on what Shmebecca had told them, and how she had asked for help to sabotage Mr. Eyebrows's plan.

"Could we get in trouble for that?" Jennizabeth asked. "They'd probably send us back home if they caught us, right?"

"I think it'd be much, much worse than that," Candelabra said.

Bobert frowned at her. "You think?"

"I guess it depends on what the plan is, exactly. But if there's any kind of crime, it could become a diplomatic incident. The king of Nefaria might have to get involved, and the Interkingdom Department of Crimes and Stuff would definitely investigate us."

"That all sounds very serious," Stanbert said. He kicked at a rock on the ground, though it turned out to be a rock-shaped fur ball, which was a kind of animal. He apologized to it as it rolled away muttering curses.

"Look, we don't know exactly what the plan is yet. If you two would rather not help Shmebecca, that's okay," Bobert said. "But Candelabra and I are going to." He looked at her and nodded, and she wondered if he could see the hesitation on her face. She tried to nod resolutely like he had, hoping that would hide the fact that she wasn't sure she was willing to get in trouble for Shmebecca. What if they went to jail? What if she never got to see Sandraliere again? What good would lasagnanite do if she couldn't—Candelabra stopped herself from going down that line of thinking. The fact of the matter was that this wasn't a land of evil schemes, no matter how schemey Mr. Eyebrows seemed. Then why was it so hard to express her doubts to Bobert?

"I didn't even get to help on the *last* scheme's sabotage," Jennizabeth said.

They all turned to look at Stanbert to complete the circle. He rolled his eyes so hard that Candelabra was surprised they didn't go sliding down his face. "What else am I going to do? Just hang out and have corn dogs?"

"Those corn dogs *were* really good," Candelabra said, her voice coming out almost like a whisper.

The others laughed, thinking it was a joke. Under normal circumstances, it might have been. She let them think it was, that she was just lightening the mood before taking down another evil scheme. But a small part of her wasn't all that interested in the plan Shmebecca was about to lay out for them. She wanted to be back at the natural springs, enjoying the beauty of this new kingdom and all that it might be able to offer her.

11

EVERY INCH OF THE PICNIC TABLES WAS COVERED UP WITH paper of some sort. There were a handful of lists meticulously written in what Candelabra assumed was Shmebecca's handwriting. There was also a map of the region of Joviala they were in, and what looked to be at least three sets of blueprints. Shmebecca was standing at the end of one table with her hands on her hips, studying the blueprints. Two kids who Candelabra assumed were Shmebecca's friends were playing some complicated game that involved clapping their hands and then flicking each other. They both had shoulder-length black hair and were wearing matching floral jumpsuits and glasses, and when they turned to look at Candelabra, she got the sense that they were related, even though their skin tones were several shades apart and their faces weren't all that similar.

"Hey," the one on the right said, with an easy smile that made Candelabra instantly want to be friends with her.

Before any of the Nefarians could respond, Shmebecca clapped her hands loudly. "We'll all get to know each other soon enough," she said. "For now we have to figure out how to ruin the plan to move the mountain." She nodded at the many papers on the picnic table, as if they'd had a chance to process any of them.

"I'm guessing there's supposed to be a plan hidden in here somewhere?" Stanbert said, lifting up the paper closest to him and inspecting it. "What am I looking at—is this the inside of a nose?"

Shmebecca snatched the paper away from him. "That's a diagram of Mount Saint Helenhunt." She studied it lovingly for a second, then handed it back to Stanbert. "Actually, you should all study it. I'll take it to the village copycat to make copies for all of you."

"What's a copycat?" Bobert asked.

"It's a cat that makes copies of stuff," said the kid who'd smiled at Candelabra. "You don't have them in Nefaria?"

"Not that I know of. We have mimic gophers, but they just kind of make fun of how people walk."

Shmebecca clapped her hands again to get their attention. "No distractions, please! I don't want to exaggerate, but this is maybe the most important thing any of us will ever do for as long as we live."

Candelabra bit her lip, deciding not to object. She knew that stressful situations made people prone to outrageous statements.

"Okay," Shmebecca continued, when the group quieted down. "Here's what I have so far." She took a deep breath, like she was about to swim a long distance under water. "Basically, what they're doing now is digging as deep as they can across the base of the mountain with normal digging machines." She pointed at the bottom of the diagram of Mount Saint Helenhunt. Then she shuffled around for some other papers until she found one that showed what looked like a drawing of two big hands with wheels. Candelabra recognized the machines from the construction site at the base of the mountain. "They have about six of these that just dig all that dirt and rocks and stuff out. But they can't get through the bedrock. So that's when they'll switch to . . ."

Shmebecca dropped the diagram of the digger and shuffled around the pile of papers until she found what looked like one of those very long receipts they gave at apothecaries. "Explosives!" she said.

"Where did you get that?" Shmebecca's smiley friend asked, reaching for it. It turned out her name was Shmayden, and the other one, who was her cousin, was named Shmelix.

Shmebecca handed the receipt over and continued without

bothering to answer. "But they don't plan on just blowing up the whole mountain. That would take too long and—"

"They'd have a ton of rubble to deal with." Shmayden finished the sentence for her. "And rubble attracts rubble-rousers, which are these giant snakes that live around here and eat rubble. That would be a guaranteed disaster."

"Exactly! So it looks like they're planning on separating the mountain from the ground and physically moving it." Shmebecca was on a roll now, her hands gesturing all over the place and her hair coming undone from her ponytail. "Which means they need some pretty strong magic, probably extremely enchanted equipment of one sort or another." She started flipping through papers even more quickly now, at times looking like she knew exactly where on the picnic tables to look, and at times looking like she was just pretending to sift through papers, like when a teacher called out Candelabra for not having her homework and she had to act like she had no idea how it had gotten lost.

"So, I went through some records and found a handful of ways they could do it. There's elevator shmelevators, of course," Shmebecca continued, speaking so quickly that Candelabra was impressed she still had any breath left in her lungs. "But *those* are currently being used to build a dam on the Weehee! River near the border with Infamia. Unless Mr. Eyebrows is planning on moving the mountain in three years when that project is done, I don't think they're what we're looking for. That leaves two options. One is the Cursed Strong Woman of Los Angsteles. But, according to this article from *Variety* I found in the library, she's committed to filming a movie for the next three months—"

"What's a movie?" Jennizabeth said.

"We can keep an eye on that," Shmebecca continued. Candelabra offered her friend a shrug as they listened. "But everything about this operation on the mountain so far tells me it's happening soon. As soon as possible. That leaves only . . ." She reached into her backpack and pulled out a rolled-up paper.

"So none of *these* papers were the important one?" Stanbert muttered before being shushed by no fewer than three people.

Shmebecca unfurled the paper, which took up almost the entire table. Candelabra squinted and then turned her head to try to make sense of what she was looking at. This one wasn't a diagram, but a painting. The item depicted kind of looked like a tree, with a long trunk and a big bushy top. With blueberries in it, maybe?

"No way!" everyone called out.

Shmebecca was standing with her hands on her hips and a very satisfied expression. "You guys know about the Muffin of Glory?"

"I wrote my essay about it," Candelabra said.

"Most of us did," Jennizabeth added. At the interested looks of the Jovialese, she shrugged. "Mr. Gigglebutt gave us a choice. Natural disasters and a happy history of no evil schemes weren't really interesting to us. But a magical pastry that is one of the most powerful devices across all the kingdoms?"

"It was the only essay I've ever enjoyed writing," Stanbert cut in. "So cool."

Shmebecca nodded. "Okay, then, we're all on the same page. Good. I thought about it a lot, and it seems like the muffin is the only way they could gather enough energy to lift an entire mountain. But to contain that much magical power, you need this." She pointed at the trunk section of the painting, which was golden. Now that Candelabra got a closer look, she could see it was etched with ornate curlicues.

"Do you know what this is?" They all nodded their heads. It was the Scepter of Pretty Good Control, which Candelabra had read about for her essay. It tapped into the muffin's powers and harnessed all that magic so it could be used more effectively. "Great, this'll save time, then," Shmebecca said.

Again she shuffled around the picnic table, looking for some document or the other, which this time she located impressively quickly. "I found this in the records office."

Bobert reached for the document, and while he read it, searching for the pertinent information, Candelabra took a moment to look around. More and more people were arriving for the bonfire, though no one really seemed to notice the group of kids gathered around the picnic tables.

Candelabra bit her lip. Again, part of her wanted to just wrap all this up so she could keep enjoying herself, maybe talk a little with Shmayden and Shmelix, the not-twins. She'd barely been able to talk to anyone in Joviala who wasn't Shmebecca. Then she caught Bobert's eye, and he raised his eyebrows a little. She forced herself to focus.

"Okay, so it seems like Mr. Eyebrows and the Fun Corporation applied for permission to join the muffin and the scepter a couple of months ago and were approved," Bobert said, passing the paper over to Candelabra so she could read it too. She pretended to scan the page before passing it along to Shmayden.

"Right," Shmebecca said. "Even though there aren't evil schemes here, the Interkingdom Department of Magical Affairs requires that the muffin and the scepter be kept apart for security purposes. And no matter how much construction Mr. Eyebrows orders, they can't move the mountain until they have the muffin."

"So all we have to do is stop the muffin and the scepter from being joined?" Stanbert asked, scratching his head.

"Exactly!" Shmebecca shouted. While she'd been explaining everything so breathlessly, her hair tie had come undone to the point that it was basically just sitting on top of her head now. And even though the sun had dipped over the horizon, Candelabra could see how bright red the girl's cheeks were. "They already borrowed the scepter a week ago from the Googlyeyes Museum. We have two days to stop them from getting the muffin. It's on one of these other papers," she said, gesturing vaguely at the table.

"How are we supposed to do that?" Shmelix said.

"I'm still figuring that part out." Shmebecca shuffled a few papers about, searching for who knew what. As she did, she uncovered a sheet that called out to Candelabra for some reason. She reached for it as Shmebecca sighed. "Do any of you know any ghosts?"

"I do," Bobert said, raising his hand. "But she's back in Nefaria, and she's not actually scary." He furrowed his brow then added, "Unless you're afraid of conversations. She's really chatty."

"Maybe she can talk them out of the whole plan!" Jennizabeth said, bursting into laughter. The others laughed along, and Candelabra sensed them all taking this a little too easily. She knew there was one way to make them reconsider.

"What happens if we get caught?" Candelabra asked.

They quieted down, and Shmebecca took a deep breath. "Well," she said, "From what I can tell from the news articles I've read, the interkingdom departments don't like people who mess with magical artifacts under their control."

THE GREATEST HEIST IN JOVIALA

"What does that mean?" Stanbert asked. "If we get caught they punish us? They feed us to dragons?"

"No," Shmebecca said quickly. Then she reached for the top of her head, grabbed her tie, and wrapped her hair back up in a loose knot that almost immediately started coming undone. "I mean, they did that once, yes. But it wasn't kids—it was some sentient dragon kibble that had gotten the taste for human flesh and had already eaten an entire village."

"So if we don't eat a village, we should be okay?" Bobert offered.

"I don't want to lie. It's hard to know for sure. But they probably would charge us with crimes." She rubbed her nose. "Hopefully not a lot of them. I don't know which ones, though." Again, she rubbed her nose, and Candelabra was reminded of the look Sandraliere got sometimes when she told her that everything inside the painting was fine. That she was happy there. "Probably a lot of them."

Before Candelabra could examine the look much further, a bell rang from inside the school, followed by a bugle call announcing that the bonfire was set to begin.

Shmebecca heaved another big sigh. "I guess that's enough for now," she said, sounding defeated. She reached to roll up the blueprints nearby, and Candelabra closed her fist, remembering the piece of paper she'd reached for. It seemed to be a business-license application for the distribution of lasagnanite.

She tried as nonchalantly as she could to slide the sheet of paper into her pocket. Thankfully, everyone else started helping Shmebecca gather all the papers, and in the rustling her thievery went unnoticed. Not that she was stealing this, or that it even belonged to Shmebecca, necessarily. She would give it back. She just needed time to read it in private.

"Let's keep brainstorming," Shmebecca added. "If you think of anything, anything at all, you can come find me at the bonfire, or at my house, or in my room—I don't care. We need to act quickly."

"How quickly?" Shmayden asked.

"Maybe tomorrow night," Shmebecca answered without hesitation. "The day after at the latest. The permit says that the Fun Corporation will be responsible for it starting in two days, so it'll be here by then. I just need to find out exactly when it's arriving. Once they have the muffin and the scepter, it'll be much harder to stop them."

Shmebecca studied the last paper on the table, which was a large map of Joviala. Mount Saint Helenhunt was prominently featured in the center of the map, and toward the bottom edge was the border of Nefaria. Everything Candelabra knew. In her pocket, she played with the edge of the paper she had stolen.

12

Bobert was sitting on a log while the group roasted swampmallows over the huge fire. It was mesmerizing to stare into, especially with a mountain-saving mission on the brain.

"Bobert, your swampmallow's totally on fire," Jennizabeth said, tapping him on the knee.

"That's how I like them," he lied, pulling his stick out and blowing on the flaming treat at the end. It was burned to a black crisp. He waited until Jennizabeth wasn't looking and tossed it back into the fire.

Then he got up to get a new swampmallow, taking a moment to look around as he headed to the snack table. Most of the Jovialese kids were running around and playing, taking advantage of the entertainment the school had set up for the visiting Nefarians. Everyone seemed pretty happy to have Shmebecca entertain them, since she was one of the host families. Although Bobert did catch a lot of the Jovialese kids looking over at him and then giggling. Probably just kids gossiping.

    He turned away, not liking the feeling. It reminded him of being in the castle during his curse, when everyone blamed him for a failed escape plan. Before that whole ordeal, Bobert had been invisible to the world, and he had hated it. But he hadn't liked being hyper-visible, either. He'd finally landed exactly where he liked, with his group of friends, being seen the perfect amount.

    He scanned the area for Candelabra. Throughout the bonfire, Bobert had been aware of her taking laps around the edge of the yard, keeping to herself. Now he saw that she was also heading toward the snack table, though absentmindedly. He went toward her, stepping around a group of Jovialese kids standing in a circle, sharing tips on how to make the perfect s'mless (a treat consisting of a swampmallow smushed between melty chocolate and some broccoli).

    As he approached Candelabra, he saw her taking something out of her pocket and studying it.

    "What ya got there?" he asked.

    Startled, Candelabra shoved the piece of paper into her pocket. "What?" She took a step back, then squinted through the dark. "Oh, hey, Bobert."

    "You okay? You've been alone since the bonfire started."

    "Yeah!" she exclaimed, her voice rising in so high a pitch she almost sounded like one of those rat-birds squeaking. "All the way okay." She chuckled and then made finger guns at Bobert.

"Finger guns?"

Candelabra sighed and dropped her hands. "Yeah, sorry, that was weird. I know we swore never to do those again." She took a few steps closer to him, then turned her attention to a row of cookies on the snack table. She picked up one that was dotted with bright green flecks and gave it a sniff, wrinkling her nose. "Cheese? Weird." She took a bite and then nodded approvingly and offered it to Bobert.

He took the cookie but held off on biting into it. "You sure you're okay?"

Candelabra bit her lip and looked off into the distance. Something flashed across her face, some emotion he couldn't recognize. Worry, maybe? Bobert had never known Candelabra to be worried, even in the face of an evil scheme. He thought maybe it could be guilt, but that didn't make sense either. What would she have to feel guilty about?

And maybe he could have simply asked her. But he didn't. Instead he asked her how she felt about Shmebecca's plan. "I think it's pretty good, but I'm sure you have some great ideas about how we can pull it off, right?"

Still, Candelabra kept staring off into the distance, slowly chewing. He had to tap her on the shoulder for her to meet his eyes again. "No," she said quietly. "I don't."

This was a different version of his friend. Normally, Candelabra would have been thrilled to talk about taking down any evil scheme. Something had changed in her since the town hall. He didn't know what, or why. Was she worried about the repercussions if they got caught? It didn't sound like her, but it was a possibility.

But clearly, she didn't want to talk about the scheme right now.

Bobert grabbed a few swampmallows and slid them onto his roasting stick, trying to think of what else he could talk to his friend about, what joke he could crack that would make things between them feel like they always did.

But he didn't have to sit with the new feelings very long. Just then another earthquake shook the ground, making the cookies on the snack table rattle on their plates. Bobert could hear his friends shriek, along with Mr. Gigglebutt, who'd been talking to Miss Petunias at the other end of the table, near the drinks.

Miss Petunias bolted away, and Bobert—who was just kind of standing with knees bent, trying to ride out the shaking—watched her grab a fire extinguisher and rush to the bonfire. Beside him, Candelabra had snapped back to the present and was holding on to the table for balance. "You okay?" he asked her again.

THE GREATEST HEIST IN JOVIALA

Now she at least offered a smile while she nodded, and Bobert decided to believe her.

As the earthquake continued, most of the Jovialese looked unbothered, which made Bobert feel a little more at ease.

Calmest of all was Shmebecca. She was sitting with Jennizabeth and Stanbert by the bonfire, her arms crossed in front of her chest. She was staring into the night without moving a muscle, the expression in her eyes as fiery as the flames Imogene Petunias was trying to extinguish.

13

SIX MORE EARTHQUAKES STRUCK JOVIALA THAT NIGHT. Most people slept right through them, or they reached out to steady the glass of water on the nightstand so it wouldn't tip over and then went right back to sleep.

Shmebecca, though, never managed to get to sleep. Right when she got over the pounding heartbeat one earthquake had caused and calmed herself enough to close her eyes again, then another one would strike. She was not worried about the house falling to pieces around her; most buildings in Joviala were designed to withstand not only earthquakes but hurricanes, floods, and even snake stampedes, among all the other natural disasters. She'd slept through many of them before, and much stronger ones at that.

Her worries had entirely to do with her mountain and the atrocities planned for it.

Since Shmorris and Shborris were sleeping in her room and she couldn't turn the lights on, after the third earthquake

Shmebecca took the pile of papers she'd gathered for her plan and went downstairs. She thought about lighting the fireplace, but that wasn't the smartest idea with increased earthquake activity.

It was a nice night out, and their front porch had a partial view of Mount Saint Helenhunt. So she carried all her papers out there with a small lantern and a mug of lavender tea. Each time the ground shook—or each time she even imagined it shaking—she cupped her hands around the tea and kept her eye on the peak that was barely visible in the dark. Then she'd set the mug down and get back to looking at all the schematics and documents she'd gathered.

In a notebook she started writing every idea she had, no matter how crazy. One was to destroy all the equipment, but she didn't know how long that would take, and it was likely that Mr. Eyebrows could just get his machines fixed or replaced. She only briefly considered kidnapping Mr. Eyebrows, but dismissed the idea because it felt highly illegal, and difficult, and she wasn't even sure if that would stop the Fun Corporation.

She wondered how things worked in other kingdoms, where there were evil schemes. Shmebecca used her wizard tablet to read about the criminal capers of Nefaria and elsewhere. She even found an article about a scheme involving a gumball machine, where the accompanying portrait showed kids who looked just like Bobert and Candelabra. She would have to ask them about it, and if they'd learned anything that could be useful.

After everything she wrote, though, the plan always came back to the Muffin of Glory, and the need to keep it from falling into Mr. Eyebrows's hands. But how? She doodled. She made schematics, scribbled lists, drew circles on maps, reread every paper in front of her, got up to get more tea, and did it all over again.

At around four in the morning, she found something on her wizard tablet. It was an announcement for a special train arriving to Joviala in the middle of the night carrying a magical item. She clicked around and found that the train was exceptionally heavy, and would be accompanied by interkingdom officials. This had to be the muffin.

Her heart started beating, and an idea popped into her head. She started writing furiously, ruffling through all the papers she had as the vision came together. Since she was a girl of science, Shmebecca had almost never experienced a moment of creative inspiration quite like this. There'd only been the time when she'd decided to recreate her beloved Mount Saint Helenhunt in mosaic form using pieces of the mountain itself.

Once her plan took shape, she went back and made little adjustments, shifting responsibilities from one kid to another, drawing diagrams that were only slightly different from previous diagrams. She tried to think of every possible wrinkle, every obstacle that might come up and threaten the plan.

There was also the little matter of consequences. Joviala, with its general lack of evildoing, took a rehabilitative approach to crime. So Shmebecca and her friends might have to go to a special school for a few years. The worst-case scenario was that her parents would receive a fine from the Interkingdom Department of Crimes and Stuff.

The Nefarians, though, wouldn't be as lucky. Shmebecca had read about all the punishments that even young prisoners were subject to in Nefaria. Not to mention the fact that they let other kingdoms add on punishments too. They called it a deterrent to scheming and crimes, but to Shmebecca it just seemed like cruelty.

Either way, stealing magical artifacts was punishable by up to ten years doing chores in a dungeon, and if the judge was particularly mean, Bobert, Candelabra, and the others might even have to do those chores while wearing a really scratchy wool turtleneck.

But Shmebecca wasn't going to let it come to that. So there was no need to warn the Nefarians, really.

By the time the sky started to bruise with the morning, Shmebecca felt confident that she'd thought about her plan to perfection. Or at least thought about it so much that it hurt to think any more. She couldn't tell if there was a difference. She convinced herself they were all going to save the mountain and get away with it, too.

"You haven't been out here all night, have you, hon?" Her dad stepped out, wearing that embarrassing combination of a robe, shin-high socks, and sandals. He took a sip of coffee and inhaled an exaggerated whiff of fresh morning air. Most people in Joviala did that, but her dad seemed especially committed to the ritual. He looked out at the sunrise and smiled like there wasn't anything in the world that could possibly worry him.

Shmebecca stifled a yawn and shrugged as a response. She didn't feel the need to lie, but she didn't want to go into details, either. After all, her parents had been there during the town hall, and afterward they hadn't been scared like she was. They'd tried to calm her down, saying that sometimes the world worked in complicated ways, and that didn't necessarily mean there was a reason to be afraid or angry. Her parents were Jovialese, after all. And like all Jovialese except her, they always believed everything would turn out okay in the end.

"What about things changing?" Shmebecca had pleaded. "What about those things Bobert and Candelabra overheard? What about the fact that it's the Fun Corporation again?"

But her parents hadn't been convinced there was anything to worry about, so they definitely wouldn't approve of the plan

THE GREATEST HEIST IN JOVIALA

Shmebecca had put together and was going to put into action that night.

Bobert came out then, eating a bowl of cereal, his hair sticking out every which way. He waved at Shmebecca, then took a bite, looking out at the pink morning light crawling its way down the mountain peak. There was a smattering of dark puffs in the sky that could have been volcanic exhalations, or they could have just been clouds.

"What do they have planned for you kiddos today?" Shmebecca's dad asked.

Bobert ran through the itinerary of museums and other sights they were being ferried to. Thankfully, they had the afternoon and evening free to spend time with their host families. Shmebecca wondered how she was going to make it through the day at school until then, when she could tell them her plan.

When her dad went back inside, Shmebecca asked Bobert if the earthquakes scared him.

"I didn't really feel them," he answered. "I might have woken up for one, but I kind of thought that was Shmorris or Shborris snoring in the other room." He took a few spoonfuls of his cereal, only now appearing to notice the notebook and the pile of papers next to her.

"I talked to our science teacher last night at the bonfire," he said. "I asked him about moving a mountain, just because

I wanted to know how dangerous it is. He said there would likely need to be a volcanic-stabilizing spell involved, even if the volcano is dormant. In case that's helpful. He also said you need a whole lot of magic for a spell of that size."

Shmebecca grabbed her notebook and jotted that down, then looked at the diagram and her plan and chewed on her pen. "It's good to know," she said. "Do you know any wizards or witches who could help with spells, if we needed them to?"

"Um. Kind of. But I don't think he'd be very helpful. He's kind of in jail. And evil." Bobert scratched his head and seemed to notice that his hair was doing strange things, so he started combing it down with his fingers. "I don't think we should try to use him."

"That's okay." Shmebecca was on her feet now, mind churning. "It's good to know." She paced back and forth. "I already have a good plan. Knowing about that spell is just icing on the cake." And now, saying it out loud, looking at her plan written out, it felt like she'd really landed on something. She almost wanted to hug Bobert. Instead she gathered her papers into a neat pile. "Tell everyone to meet at the picnic table again at sundown. We might be able to save my mountain."

When she looked up to beam at Bobert, she noticed Candelabra at the door right behind him. The door was cracked, so she would have been able to hear Shmebecca. It even looked like she had been on her way out to join them. Their eyes met for the briefest of moments, and Candelabra quickly glanced away. But Shmebecca waved her over, and after hesitating for a second, Candelabra joined them outside.

"Morning," she said softly.

"Hey. You look like you didn't sleep great," Shmebecca said. "Earthquakes keep you up?"

Candelabra ran a hand through her hair, which was still matted from sleep. "I guess so, yeah," she said. She looked over at the papers Shmebecca had been working on but didn't ask about them. Instead she blew warm air into her hands and then sat on them.

Shmebecca leaned over her chair to reach into the wicker basket nearby where they kept all the blankets. She pulled out a red checkered one and handed it to Candelabra.

"Oh, thanks," Candelabra said, taking the blanket like she was surprised by it. She was probably still just waking up. "That's really nice of you."

"Of course!" Shmebecca said. "Bobert and I were just talking about—"

"The mountain, yeah," Candelabra said. "I heard. Can we . . . not? Just for a little bit? It's early, and I don't really want to think about . . . schemes right now." Candelabra gave a little chuckle and then yawned, though a part of Shmebecca felt like it wasn't a real yawn.

"Yeah, okay," Shmebecca said. She opened her mouth to

add one last thought about the plan, but then thought better of it. Candelabra seemed like she really needed to just look out at the Jovialese landscape and take a deep breath like Shmebecca's dad had done. And since she was Shmebecca's sister for the week, she decided to give her that.

14

FOR SHMEBECCA, IT WAS A VERY LONG DAY OF WAITING. She'd been sneaking out to the library, and holding on through even more earthquakes, hoping that her plan wouldn't be too little too late. She kept her eye on the mountain as often as possible, afraid that at any moment she would see it simply disappear. Every now and then she could hear an explosion coming from that direction, and just picturing the construction equipment (and the destruction equipment) got her antsy to go and tear it all down.

Now, finally, as the afternoon light turned golden, she saw the others arriving at the picnic tables.

Bobert, Stanbert, and Jennizabeth were walking in a group. Candelabra was a few steps behind, looking at her feet. Shmelix and Shmayden were coming up just behind her, the only two of Shmebecca's own friends who'd agreed to come. She had tried to recruit a few more classmates throughout the day, but it turned out that all that time spent by herself on the mountain had resulted in her not having that many friends she could ask for a favor. Especially not one of this magnitude. Most people were sick of hearing her talk about the mountain anyway.

That was okay, though. She had the Nefarians, and having *too* many people might make the plan fall apart by attracting too much attention. She'd hoped for at least ten kids total, but seven would have to do. A small part of her couldn't help but think of what Mr. Eyebrows had said at the town hall: all those references to fun. She wondered if maybe she didn't choose to have fun enough in her life. But she rejected the thought immediately. Her mountain was a place where she had fun. It might not have looked like the over-the-top depictions of fun that were on Mr. Eyebrows's posters, but that didn't mean there wasn't fun to be found there.

As they approached the table, Shmebecca's heart started feeling like it was pumping magma through her veins. Not necessarily in a bad way. Just that she had this incredible energy within her. She wondered if her mountain ever felt that way. If it was feeling that way now.

She took a breath, remembering that volcanoes that exhaled a little at a time were much less likely to blow up. And now was not the time to blow up.

Everyone was chatting about their day as they gathered around the picnic table like they had the night before.

Candelabra was the only silent one, picking at a corner of the wooden table.

Shmebecca waited for them to get out the last of the conversation, knowing she was about to ask a lot of them, and deciding it was best to let them feel like everything was normal for at least a few more seconds. Rather than her pile of papers, she had just her notebook in her hands, and she flipped through it absentmindedly.

Since Candelabra was the only silent one, Shmebecca stood next to her and quietly asked her if she'd had a good day.

Candelabra seemed surprised by the question, almost as if she hadn't even noticed Shmebecca standing there. She tucked her golden hair behind her ear and said, "What?" Then she added, "Oh yeah, it was . . . great, actually. I really like Joviala." She smiled, then averted her eyes like she'd just said something embarrassing.

"Good," Shmebecca said. "Me too. That's why I'm trying to save it. And thanks for helping."

Candelabra smiled again but didn't meet Shmebecca's eyes.

That was when Shmebecca realized that the group had naturally quieted down, at which point Shmelix looked at her and asked, "So, the grappling hook you asked me to bring—what's it for?"

Surprisingly, Shmebecca found herself smiling, all the heat of the magma in her veins turning from nervous energy to excitement. She was doing this. They were doing this. "That's in case we need to enter the train from above," she said.

"What train?" Shmayden asked.

"The train that's carrying the Muffin of Glory." She waited for them to ask a bunch of follow-up questions, but a silence fell over the group as they all shot looks at one another. It was a little disappointing, if she was being honest. "Does anyone want to ask what we're going to do with the train and the grappling hook?"

"It sounds like we're going to steal the muffin from the train," Stanbert mumbled.

"Yeah, I was guessing steal it," Bobert said. There was a chorus of agreement from everyone else.

"Oh," Shmebecca said, even more disappointed that she hadn't gotten to say it. Then she realized that none of them were running away from her kooky idea. No one was even complaining. "Um, is that okay with everyone?"

"I'm still in," Shmelix said resolutely, nodding his head.

"Can we go over the bad stuff again?" Stanbert asked. "What happens if we get caught?"

"We're not going to get caught," Shmebecca said quickly, raising her voice as if saying it loudly would make it true.

"We don't know that," Candelabra answered. The others quieted down.

Shmebecca wasn't sure if she was imagining it, but she

thought she could hear explosions in the distance. No one else was looking at Candelabra. The two girls' eyes met, and Shmebecca was surprised at the fear she saw in her new friend's eyes. It made sense. The chance that she'd get caught doing something bad while on a trip in a strange land, the punishment that might follow. Shmebecca knew that it wasn't the same for the Nefarians, knew that they were used to people getting punished all the time. If there was any time to tell them the specific punishment they'd face if they did get caught, it was now.

Instead Shmebecca cleared her throat and then offered her most reassuring smile. "I've thought about this a lot. We're not going to get caught," she said. Then, without thinking much about it, she added, "If we do, I'll take all the blame."

Candelabra looked away.

Stanbert raised his hand as if he was in class. "Can I be the one who uses the grappling hook?"

"Wait, no fair, I want a chance too. Can we both use it?" Bobert said, also raising his hand.

Stanbert and Bobert, their hands still raised, started talking at the same time, arguing about how they would each like a shot, and that maybe there was a fairer way than calling dibs. Maybe something called rock-paper-scissors.

"What is that?" Shmayden asked.

"It's a game we play in Nefaria when we can't decide who gets to do something," Bobert said. "Like this." He held out one hand flat with his palm turned outward while using his other hand to make a fist; then he held his fingers out like scissors and kind of karate-chopped his open hand.

"Oh," Shmayden said. "We have that game. But we call it fist-fingers-slap."

Stanbert tilted his head. "What beats what?"

"Slap usually wins," Shmelix said with a shrug.

"Can we get back to the plan, please? If we're going to do this, we need to get started," Shmebecca said, looking nervously up at the setting sun. She explained the plan she'd spent all night coming up with:

The special train carrying the magical item was going to bypass the station in town at around midnight, taking an old cargo route that ran closer to the construction site near Mount Saint Helenhunt. Which was perfect, because it was far away from prying eyes. By the time the train reached Mr. Eyebrows and his destructive crew, the muffin would already be gone.

Shmebecca showed them the diagram she'd drawn of the train, pointing at the middle car, where the special cargo was likely to be held, since it was super heavy (it was a very dense muffin) and putting it at either end could derail the train. There were various entry points throughout the train, but the best was either from the top (hence the grappling hook) or the nearest car.

If the train was moving fast, they would have to create a distraction on the tracks to get the engineer to slow down, which would then put security on alert. Maybe the most surprising thing was that there *was* security in the kingdom of Joviala. It just proved how powerful the muffin was, and that other kingdoms didn't want it falling into the wrong hands.

Because of the security team, the kids would have to board the train at the right time, without creating too much of a fuss. Then they had to incapacitate the guards. Anticipating the questions about how exactly they were going to do that, Shmebecca brought out the sleeping potions she'd bought at the apothecary, along with a Night-Night stick, a weighted blanket, a length of rope, a handful of knotted shoelaces she'd found in her parents' closet, a set of toy handcuffs the twins used to play with all the time, and a magical instant-hatch chicken egg.

"How is that one going to help?" Candelabra asked.

"I don't know, but it's easy to carry, so I figured it was worth bringing," Shmebecca answered, continuing before more discussion could break out. Once they had incapacitated the guards, the muffin wouldn't just be sitting there for them to grab. It was encased in Unbreakable Glass™ and submerged in an aquarium with electric piranhas, which, contrary to popular to belief, didn't like to eat people. But they *were* very angry fish that didn't like to be disturbed—not to mention the whole electricity thing.

If they managed to get past the fish without losing any limbs, there was still the fact of the muffin's weight to deal with. It famously needed the strength of ten warriors to carry it.

"Perfect," Stanbert muttered. "Seven children. Ten warriors. Same difference."

Shmebecca cleared her throat and continued. "Once we have it, we'll need to get off the train again without getting caught, then hide the muffin somewhere it won't be found until Mr. Eyebrows is forced to cancel the project." She paused. She'd rehearsed saying this part, though now it felt unnecessarily dramatic. "Which maybe means we have to hide it forever."

"I guess that doesn't sound too terrible," Bobert said.

Stanbert laughed. "Yeah, sure, we'll just take turns keeping it in each other's pockets. What part of this plan sounds like something we can do?"

Bobert scratched his head and shrugged. "I dunno. At least there's not, like, a curse attached to it or anything," he said.

"Oh, about that," Shmebecca said, grimacing as she remembered. "I couldn't find anything confirming it, but there are rumors that anyone who touches the glass encasing the muffin gets cursed."

"Poop," Bobert said, scrunching his nose up. "What's the curse?"

"Something about facing your deepest fears without ever being able to stop being afraid of them."

"Is that it?" Jennizabeth said, with a sarcastic scoff.

Another silence set in, so complete that Shmebecca was sure everyone could hear her gulping nervously. She hadn't exactly made it sound like a great idea to do what she was suggesting they do. Not that she had anything better to add. There was more, but it wouldn't help anyone.

"Are we sure this is worth it?" Candelabra asked, her voice just above a whisper. "Maybe Adventure Land won't be so bad."

Shmebecca couldn't blame her for asking. And for the first time, she had doubts about whether she should be dragging all these kids into this ridiculous adventure with her. "I won't be angry if any of you decide to leave," she said. "But I believe that we have to stop this project. An amusement park isn't worth risking the mountain—and the Fun Corporation has proved to us that this *is* a risk. They have no idea what the consequences of meddling with nature like this could be. They admitted it themselves!" Shmebecca puffed out her cheeks as she exhaled. "This is what they do. They're careless and they hurt people, and that's what they're doing to the whole kingdom."

She groaned and stepped away from the table to calm herself down. It felt like she was back in the mud. Except now it was the mountain in there, and she couldn't repay the favor. If her mountain disappeared, how would she ever feel safe again? The others couldn't see her face, but she still wiped at her eyes. She breathed in long and slow, trying not to picture the mountain gone already.

She turned back to the group. "If any of you have to leave, I understand. I'm still going to try. Even if it's just me."

Jennizabeth chuckled, and Shmebecca was glad to see that all the others were as confused as she was. When no one said anything, Jennizabeth rolled her eyes and then looked over at Candelabra. "You gave almost the exact same speech last year! Before we went to rescue Bobert."

Candelabra looked down at the ground. "No, I didn't," she mumbled. Was Shmebecca imagining things, or was Candelabra looking pale, as if she might faint at any second?

"What's with you today?" Jennizabeth asked. Then she turned to Shmebecca. "Anyway, we're all still in. Just tell us what to do."

That was exactly what Shmebecca wanted to hear. She gave one more glance at Candelabra, who was picking at the table with her fingernail. Even though it seemed like she wanted to run away, she stayed still. Shmebecca breathed a sigh of relief.

Their schedule called for a dinner with their host families, but Shmebecca had convinced her parents that what the visitors needed was to eat in town with no adults around. Stanbert and Jennizabeth's host family had agreed to let them go, so the group had a few hours of freedom. The train was scheduled to come through at midnight, so they would have time to figure out the plan, then go home for a quick rest before sneaking back out. In the meantime, sticking around at the picnic tables by school would only arouse suspicion, so they had to go somewhere they could hammer out the final details in peace. The bog at the foot of Mount Saint Helenhunt was Shmebecca's favorite place to go when she wanted some privacy. Unfortunately, after sundown it often got mud tornadoes, which were sometimes fun but might hurt and/or scare the Nefarians. Plus, it wasn't a good idea to go missing past bedtime and have people come searching for them.

Instead they had to hide in plain sight. A place where kids could gather to discuss what roles they would each have in pulling off a heist of one of the most powerful magical items without arousing the suspicion of adults.

So, off they went to the library. They took a small detour to practice throwing the grappling hook, which turned out to be much heavier than they expected. Only Candelabra managed to throw it above her head, and barely at that.

Shmebecca was glad to see that the librarian working there was Mrs. Shmobinson, who tended to let kids be. Other librarians were a little nosier.

"Welcome, Shmebecca! You brought visitors!"

"Yup," Shmebecca said, signaling for the others to go

straight to the back room. "They're from another kingdom, so I brought them here to learn about Joviala!"

"No better place to do it," Mrs. Shmobinson said. "Welcome to the best place in Joviala!"

The kids called back thank-yous and were promptly shushed by other people in the library. With so many names starting with "sh," for reasons that were unclear even to those who studied its history and language, Joviala was a pretty shushy place. But the library was one of the shushiest.

The crew gathered around a table in the farthest corner of the library. Shmelix and Shmayden grabbed the biggest books they could find and started building a privacy fort around them.

"I think that's just going to make us look more suspicious," Jennizabeth said.

"Nah, privacy forts are really common." Shmayden pointed across the room, where a group of older students had built very ornate privacy forts as they hunched over some textbooks.

"Okay, first things first," Shmebecca said. "We have to figure out duties." She pulled out the notebook where she'd jotted down the plan the night before. "Who's the fastest person here?"

"Definitely Candelabra," Bobert and Jennizabeth said.

Stanbert started to protest, but Shmebecca could tell that even he knew he wasn't as fast as Candelabra. "Okay,

Candelabra, you're gonna board the train from the back, then. You'll have to run onto it while it's moving, because there'll probably be a lookout when it's stopped. Which brings us to acting. Who thinks they can convince a train carrying one of the most important magical artifacts known to humankind to stop for them and a rat-bird?"

Once they'd all agreed on their skills and what role each would take, and after she'd double-checked their privacy fort, Shmebecca laid out the plan.

They drank the flower tea they'd bought from the café next door and snuck into the library, and went over everything minute by minute, taking turns repeating what they would have to do, until everyone could recite the plan from memory without making a mistake (or, in Stanbert's case, a bad joke). There were a few moments that threatened to break out into shouting matches, as people groaned when someone got it wrong and had to start over, the frustrations mounting as the time stretched on. Thankfully, Mrs. Shmobinson was busy trying to keep all the books on the shelves, and the privacy fort held up well despite the constant earthquakes.

After a couple of hours they were all tired and the library was about to close, but there was an air of giddiness in their corner of the library too. Bobert was downright giggly, and Shmayden and Shmelix looked as focused as when they had played in the frees-bees regional championship a few months before. Candelabra had been quiet nearly the whole evening, but Shmebecca chose to see that as a similar focus. She had taken a lot of notes, after all, which Shmebecca, as a fan of the sciences, appreciated.

"Okay, one more time," Shmebecca said.

The group groaned, but none of them gathered their things quite yet. They waited for Shmebecca to clear her throat and clap her hands, the way she'd been doing at the start of every run-through so far.

She clapped her hands. "Eleven forty-five p.m., train rolls in."

Jennizabeth was mid-yawn, but she repeated her role. "I drag a rat-bird across the tracks to get them to stop."

Shmebecca clapped again, and Bobert jumped in, unable to contain a smile. "Once the train is stopped, I use a grappling hook attached to a flying goat to get to the top of the train, since it turns out none of us are very good at throwing the grappling hook very far."

"I got pretty close," Shmayden said with a shrug.

Another clap from Shmebecca kept them from arguing again about who got closest. "Eleven forty-seven."

"I sneak onto the third car," Stanbert said.

"I enter the fourth car ready to kick some guards' butts. Or at least their shins? Some part of them that will buy us time," Shmayden said. "If I can't do it with my feet, I'll use my bag of tricks. Specifically tying their shoelaces and using our hugging snakes, which I'll have in my backpack."

"Meanwhile, I'm scanning the opposite side of the train for another entry point," Shmelix said.

Shmebecca was looking down at her notebook to make sure everyone was on the same page. A silence followed, so she clapped her hands again, not looking up right away until she heard someone whispering, "Candelabra, that's you."

Candelabra was staring off into the distance, chewing on her thumb. Everyone looked from her to Shmebecca, as if to see what she would do. A part of Shmebecca wanted to yell that this was important. She wanted to cry, thinking that her plan might not work. But then she swallowed those feelings down. She was asking a lot from her friends. And from these strangers, who were somehow bringing themselves to help her out.

She closed her notebook, and the rustling of the papers finally stirred Candelabra from whatever she was thinking about. "Sorry, is it my turn? I . . . um. I'll be, um, running behind. And then—"

"It's okay," Shmebecca interrupted her. She stood up and started gathering her things. "I think we have it. We should get some sleep while we can. It'll go much better that way." It took a second for the others to understand what she had said. Candelabra was even slower than that. She seemed frozen, almost like she wasn't in the room anymore. Shmebecca hoped she was just tired.

Shmayden broke the silence by saying, "Yay, bed," and all of them broke out into quiet chatter as they took down their privacy fort and gathered their belongings, moving slowly. Shmebecca reminded them of the rendezvous point, and then they all started filing out past the other library patrons, some of whom were still hunching over books or using wizard tablets to research either perfectly normal or way-too-weird subjects, despite Mrs. Shmobinson clearing her throat to remind them it was time to leave.

Outside the library, once everyone had said their goodbyes, Shmebecca turned to the west to lead Candelabra and Bobert home. But Candelabra said she was going to walk on her own. "I have to repeat the plan out loud for a little while," she said. "And calm my nerves. You guys go ahead. I know the way back."

"You're sure?" Shmebecca asked.

But before Candelabra could answer, another voice cut through the night. "A little late for you kids, isn't it?"

Shmebecca turned to see Miss Petunias, one of the Nefarian teachers. She was a tall, strong-looking woman, vaguely familiar, even though Shmebecca couldn't say why. She was leaning against the library wall, her arms crossed over her chest. The way she looked at them made Shmebecca feel like they were in trouble, even though they hadn't done anything. Yet.

"We were just studying!" Bobert blurted out.

Miss Petunias narrowed her eyes and nodded. "Studying," she repeated flatly. "For what?"

The silence that followed wasn't uncomfortable so much as it was an obvious stalling tactic. After ten very long seconds of staring at one another, all three kids spoke.

Bobert said, "Rocks."

Shmebecca said, "Yes."

Candelabra said, "I'll see you guys later!"

With that, Candelabra turned and speed-walked away from the three of them, her footsteps clattering on the sidewalk. Shmebecca watched her disappear into the night, slack-jawed and kind of wishing that she'd thought of running away as an option. Or that Candelabra had included them in her awkward escape plan.

Miss Petunias watched Candelabra go, then turned her attention back to Shmebecca and Bobert, raising a sly eyebrow. Shmebecca bit her lip, not wanting to say anything, afraid that they'd get caught even before the plan could kick off.

"You kids gonna be okay?" Miss Petunias asked, a slight rise in her voice, almost as if she were making a joke, even though that wasn't what the words would indicate. "Getting home, I mean."

They both nodded eagerly. "Yes, we should do that now," Shmebecca said. She grabbed Bobert's arm and led him up the street, waving goodbye to the intimidating Nefarian teacher.

"Is she onto us?" Bobert whispered when they were a safe distance away.

Shmebecca looked over her shoulder to check, and saw that Miss Petunias was staring straight at them, her arms crossed over her chest, a slight smile on her face. Then she turned on her heel and walked in the direction that Candelabra had disappeared.

15

THE TIME HAD COME.

The kids lay waiting in the bushes beside the tracks, listening for the rumble that would announce the train's arrival. Which was confusing with the ground shaking from earthquakes every ten minutes, so Bobert was mostly looking for the headlight to appear around the mountain's bend. He was also looking around in the dark for a sign of Candelabra.

When he and Shmebecca had snuck out of her house, they'd waited for Candelabra. She'd come home late after splitting up at the library and was unusually quiet. They'd agreed to meet in the woods behind Shmebecca's backyard, but Bobert had left the twins' room alone. They assumed Candelabra had snuck out early, eager to take down Mr. Eyebrows's scheme. But Bobert and Shmebecca had been the first to arrive at the group's meeting spot by the train tracks, and Candelabra still hadn't appeared.

"Where is she?" Shmebecca whispered. "The train will be here any second, and we need her."

"She'll be here," Bobert assured her. "There's nothing Candy hates more than evil schemes, trust me. Whatever she's doing is important. Maybe she thought of something that can help us carry the muffin. I've heard of magic gloves that can carry anything. Not sure where she might find them, but I could see her making a last-minute attempt to."

Even though he was saying this very confidently, Bobert wasn't entirely sure he believed it. Something had changed in Candelabra in the last day or so. He couldn't put his finger on what, exactly. The most confusing part about it all was that he thought of her as someone who thrived taking down evil schemes. She should have been at her most comfortable leading the charge alongside Shmebecca.

"I agree. I know her better than anyone, and she'll be here," Jennizabeth said. She was sitting cross-legged on the ground next to Bobert, who was crouching so he could peek through the bushes to spot the train.

Shmayden and Shmelix were building a dirt castle to keep themselves busy. Stanbert was farther off by some trees, doing a calisthenic routine to warm up. He, Bobert, and Candelabra had learned it last year when they were stuck in Matt the Evil Wizard's stupid castle, though it seemed unlikely that Matt himself had taught them the routine, and Bobert couldn't for

THE GREATEST HEIST IN JOVIALA

the life of him remember who else might have shown it to them.

There was a rustle somewhere beyond Stanbert, and Bobert swiveled his head, thinking it would be Candelabra. But no, there didn't seem to be anything. It must have been some small animal.

He didn't have too much time to think about it, because just then there was a loud tooting sound. It wasn't even coming from the mountain itself, which had been making all sorts of noises throughout the night.

"It's coming!" Shmebecca called out. "Everyone get in position!"

Bobert turned toward the tracks and saw the light reflecting off of them, growing brighter as the train rumbled closer.

"What do we do about not having Candelabra?" Jennizabeth said.

Shmebecca sighed and scanned the area, which caused her hair tie to fall to the ground. She picked it up, brushed it off, and retied her bun. "We'll have to make do," she huffed. "Stanbert, when you and Jennizabeth take down your guard, rush over to help—"

"I'm here!" Candelabra shouted, appearing from the direction of town. She was out of breath, sweat glistening on her forehead.

"Where were you?" Bobert asked, wondering if she was

okay, surprised that he was a little angry at her for being late.

"No time," Shmebecca hissed. "Candelabra, cross the tracks! It sounds like the train's going a little faster than expected, so you might have to really sprint to get on the back. Stanbert, make sure she gets on."

"You got it," he grumbled, stretching his leg out in a complicated hold that looked like it was probably bad for his knees.

Bobert had a lot of questions for Candelabra, but she was already on her way to her position, and his racing heart (and Shmebecca's quickly unraveling topknot) told him he should be getting ready too. All the others were scrambling into position, grabbing whatever item fit with their designated task.

Stanbert was slipping a black sock over his head so no one would see him when he jumped onto one of the side doors. Except it was just a child's tube sock, so he was having a hard time.

The first car held the train engineer. The second one was a sleeper car. It wasn't unusual for long-distance trains to have sleeper cars, even if they were carrying sensitive magical items. Sleep was very important no matter what kingdom, and the gentle swaying of a train was the only way some people could fall asleep. Knowing this, the kids didn't want to disturb anyone there. Not just because sleep was sacred, but because then there'd be more attention on the fact that there were kids on the train. Although, if *all* the people on the train were asleep, that would make their plan much easier.

They'd determined that Stanbert was the best at hide-and-seek, so his job was to sneak onto the third car and make his way to the middle, trying to disable guards by tying their shoelaces together (this was well known in many kingdoms to be an effective battle technique that even the greatest warriors had trouble overcoming).

The fifth car held the muffin, but had no direct access from outside the train. They were going to try to approach it from everywhere else. Shmayden would get on the fourth car, since she was the best fighter among them and more guards were likely to be there. She would also try the shoelace trick if she could, but in her backpack she'd brought her and Shmelix's hugging snakes. Bobert hadn't ever heard of them, but they were snakes that loved people so much they sometimes hugged them until the people couldn't breathe. He was going to have to ask for some as a birthday present, since they'd come in handy in any future schemes he'd face.

Other than being the fastest, Candelabra was also the best at talking to grown-ups, so she would try to use her skills to tell any guards she encountered that she was just using the bathroom, and then bonk them on the head with the Night-Night stick.

Bobert saw Shmebecca and Jennizabeth moving toward the tracks. Jennizabeth was the best actor, and even though she hadn't wanted this particular lead role at first, they'd flattered her into accepting the job of distracting the train into slowing down.

While she was pretending to herd her "pet rat-bird" across the tracks, apologizing to the engineer for the inconvenience, Bobert and Shmayden got set to use the grappling hook, which was currently attached to a flying goat, to enter the fifth car from a shaft above. Bobert had used the flying-goat call he'd learned years ago to call one over to the tracks, and he'd explained to it patiently what they needed to do. The flying goat had shrugged and made its little cooing sound, then pooped a little and gone to sleep, which they all took to mean it wanted them to wake it up when it was time for the heist to begin.

Now Bobert gently nudged the goat awake, placing the rope for the grappling hook in its mouth after it had finished stretching out in surprisingly catlike fashion. "Okay, it's time, little guy," he said. "You remember what we talked about? Fly onto the train and set the hook down so it catches on something sturdy."

The goat cooed again, then fluttered its wings. Shmayden petted the goat under its chin. She was going to help make sure Bobert was secured to the grappling hook before jumping on board the next car up.

"Please don't cause Bobert to fall, because that'll hurt a lot," Shmayden said. As if to prove it, the train now appeared around the bend. It was still somewhat far away, but Bobert could tell it was big, and moving fast. Falling from it would definitely hurt, more than "a lot."

The group was now spread out along a fifty-yard length of the tracks, most of them hiding in the brush. Only Shmebecca and Jennizabeth stood in sight of the train tracks, where they'd laid out a bunch of pillows and cloths in the shape of a rat-bird. Real rat-birds were famously honest, and it would have been hard to convince a real one to participate in their scheme.

Shmebecca lit a hand torch and started waving her hands in exaggerated motions. It was crucial that the engineer notice them and slow down, because the train was definitely moving too fast for them to board at its current speed. If it didn't slow down, the whole plan would be ruined, and the mountain would be gone by morning, leaving disaster in its wake.

As if to remind them of the stakes, the earth shook again. It was the strongest quake yet, maybe because they were right next to the mountain. Bobert looked up at it and could swear he saw it moving from side to side. There was even a puff of smoke rising from its crater, although maybe that was just a cloud.

He turned to focus on the very difficult task ahead, keeping his hand on the goat so it wouldn't fly off too early. This was definitely not what he'd expected of a field trip to Joviala, and he briefly wondered how they'd arrived here, if they'd let themselves be carried away by Shmebecca's passion for the mountain. But then he thought about what would have become of him and all those kids stuck in Matt the Wizard's cursed gumball machine last year if Candelabra hadn't cared enough to interfere. If he himself hadn't felt the drive to save them. He'd been afraid of things changing when he came here. But things were just the same as always. He drew comfort from that.

Before he could keep thinking about it, the train was upon them. It was bigger than he'd expected, bigger than any train he'd ever seen. That might have contributed to the fact that it wasn't moving quite as fast as he'd expected it to. Or maybe it had already spotted Shmebecca waving her arms, and the fake rat-bird on a leash that Jennizabeth was doing a pretty great job of pretending to try to haul away.

The train blew its horn twice, the noise reverberating in Bobert's bones. He could feel his hair blowing back. Somehow the goat beside him stayed put, starting to chew on a patch of nearby grass. For a terrifying moment, even though the train wasn't moving at top speed, it seemed like it was going to flatten the two girls.

16

M R. EYEBROWS LOVED HEARING UNEXPECTED KNOCKS on his door.

He had to admit that they initially caused him a flutter of worry and concern, but he'd long ago learned to tamp down those unpleasant emotions. He'd learned to recognize those little unexpected twists and turns to his day as what they really were: fun!

When he was little, they might have sent him scurrying to his parents' room for safety. Of course, he would find them quivering beneath the bed, barely leaving any room for him. He'd huddle close to them, drawing comfort from the heat of their bodies, even if they were shaking just as much as he was, even if the comfort didn't reach all the way through to his gut, where it was most needed.

That was a long time ago, though. "Come in!" he called.

His assistant, Shmindy, opened the door. Her hair, which

earlier had been pineapple-shaped, now took the form of a woman yawning. Shmindy used her hair mostly for decoration and as an expression of her creativity, but sometimes she used it as a hint to tell Shmebenezer that it was getting late and she wanted to go home.

"I'm sorry," he said quickly, gathering the papers on his desk into a pile. "I didn't realize how late it was. You're of course free to—"

"You have a visitor. A small one."

"How fun!" he exclaimed, unable to help himself, even though he knew that Shmindy didn't quite like children. They were hard to trust, she often said, which always made Shmebenezer laugh, even if he didn't really understand what she meant by that.

When he saw children, he often thought back to when he was a child. It wasn't an entirely pleasant thing his mind did, but it did give him a little bit of joy to realize the wholly different lives these children lived here in Joviala. They ran around on mountains, carefree, weaving in and out of trees and rat-bird herds, and even his construction site.

A flutter of excitement rushed through his stomach at the thought of the project, of the amusement park that he would bring to the children of Joviala. He was doing all this for them. Even if not all of them seemed to be entirely excited about the idea.

THE GREATEST HEIST IN JOVIALA

He cleared his throat and tamped down his enthusiasm. He drummed his fingers on his oak desk, an intentional way to dispel some of that old nervous energy. Though he wanted to focus on the fun Adventure Land would provide to the people of Joviala, he sometimes needed to work out other emotions. He didn't like those living in his head so much, and so he sent them to his fingers.

When he felt the enthusiasm overtaking everything else, he cleared his throat again. "Send them in," he said, more calmly this time, eager to discover who it was and why they had come to see him.

17

BOBERT WAS ABOUT TO SHOUT AT SHMEBECCA AND Jennizabeth to move out of the way of the train when he heard the squeal of the brakes, metal grinding against the rails.

"It's slowing down!" Stanbert called out.

"Shh!" Shmayden shushed.

Moments later, a room in the front of the train brightened with a hand torch, and a man in a striped uniform stepped out. "Hey, you kids! Get off the track," he shouted over the sound of the slowing train.

He sounded angrier than any adult Bobert had encountered in Joviala. Even Mr. Eyebrows at the town hall had been smiling the whole time that Shmebecca was trying to take down his very expensive project. Which maybe meant the engineer wasn't from Joviala at all.

Bobert chewed his lip, hoping that didn't spell trouble for the plan. Would it make it harder if the people on the train weren't from Joviala, and were therefore better at sensing trouble?

"Should we go now?" Bobert whispered.

"Not yet—wait until he's distracted."

"I'm sorry, good sir!" Jennizabeth called out in a perfectly delivered Los Angstelino accent, though Bobert wasn't sure why she was using it. That hadn't been part of the plan. Just flexing her acting muscles, he supposed. "Can you slow the train down for a moment while I convince my pet rat-bird that it's a bad idea for all of us to stay where we are?" Jennizabeth tugged at the fake leash again, very convincingly making it seem like her pet was being stubborn.

Thankfully, the train was slowing down. Not quite to a halt, but enough that Jennizabeth and Shmebecca could shout a few more things while they pretended to haul away the rat-bird-shaped sack of fabric.

Shmebecca gave her signal—she undid her hair tie—and Bobert sprang into motion. He tapped the goat twice on the back, hoping it wouldn't bray as it spread its wings out. He took a step back and watched it rise, pooping once or twice for good measure. Then it looked down at him and Shmayden, and they both gestured with their heads at the train. The second car had just rumbled past them.

All around, Bobert could make out the shapes of his friends

shuffling toward the train. In the distance Candelabra was running alongside the train's caboose and reaching for the ladder on the back. Bobert looked up at the night sky and saw that the goat was still looking down at him, flapping its little bat-like wings and smiling. "Go!" he whisper-shouted, pointing at the fifth car while still holding on to the rope of the grappling hook.

Shmayden (secondary skill: knot tying) got to work securing the rope around Bobert's waist.

It was the next car up, and if the goat landed on the wrong one, the whole plan could be ruined, since it was very likely that—aside from all the other security measures they knew about—the doors to the car and access to the muffin would be locked from the inside. The only access point was from the top of the car. Bobert was the only one small enough to fit in the vent on top of the car, and he was the group's only hope of intercepting the muffin. If the goat landed on another car, Bobert would have to jump from the roof of one car to the next, more than likely when the train was back to full speed.

Toward the front, he saw Shmebecca struggling to carry the fake rat-bird without popping off its head. Their gaze met and she widened her eyes, the question clear in her expression: *Why aren't you on the train yet?*

Stanbert was already hanging on in the space between cars

THE GREATEST HEIST IN JOVIALA

one and two. Shmelix was jumping aboard then too.

"We have to get going," Shmayden said. "The train's going to speed back up."

Bobert looked up at the goat desperately. "Come on, buddy! Now!"

The goat rolled its eyes, splattered some poop on the train, and then disappeared out of sight on the roof of the fifth car.

"You kids need a hand down there or what?" the engineer shouted to Shmebecca and Jennizabeth. "I have a schedule to stick to!"

Meanwhile, Shmayden gave a couple of tugs on the rope, which went around not just Bobert's waist but his thighs, too. "Okay, that should hold."

Bobert gulped, hoping that "should" was more confident than it sounded. "Okay," he said. "You can go."

Shmayden put a hand on his shoulder. "You've got this. Thank you for helping us." She smiled, then turned and jogged toward the front of the train to board the next car down.

Bobert felt a tug at his waist and noticed that the fifth car was starting to move past him. Shmebecca and Jennizabeth were almost off the tracks, and the train was accelerating again. He looked up and saw that the goat was staring down at him as if to say, *Well, what are you waiting for?*

He sighed, then started walking alongside the train while

he gave the rope a few jerks to make sure the goat had attached it to something secure. It seemed to hold. He took one more deep breath and reached up as high as he could on the rope, hoping that when he jumped up he would clear the train's terrifyingly large wheels. The sharp tendrils of rope cut into the palms of his hands, and he winced at what they would do to his skin when his whole body weight was focused on those tender bits of flesh. He comforted himself with the knowledge that Shmebecca had bought some healing potion at the apothecary, though he preferred not to think about how much potion he'd need if he fell from the train.

Then he jumped and started to climb as fast as he could. The train blew its horn again, and he could feel it gaining speed. He looked down at the ground, surprised at how high up he'd already made it. He caught a glimpse of Shmebecca and Jennizabeth running past him. The wind roared in his ears, though maybe that was the train itself. His hair was whipping around, stinging his eyes as he glanced at his friends. One of them said something to him, which he couldn't hear over the sounds of the train and the wind. The rope was starting to sway, bumping him into the side of the train, and he decided he didn't have time to ask them to repeat themselves.

Briefly wishing he had the climbing powers of a sloth (though maybe a little faster), Bobert focused on moving his hands up the length of the rope. He had set his feet flat on the train car and was rappelling up the side. Then the train jolted forward as it kicked into another gear, and Bobert momentarily lost his footing.

His shoulder collided with the hard metal, sending a burst of pain through his arm. Thankfully, he kept his grip on the rope, and when the pain subsided, he realized he'd almost made it to the top of the car. The goat was sitting there looking down at him, its large black eyes staring, unblinking.

"I don't suppose you could give me a hand," he grunted.

The goat tilted its head, then lifted a leg and examined its own hoof, as if pointing out to Bobert that, no, silly, it didn't have any hands. It brayed loudly.

Bobert continued his climb, and a short while later he'd gotten hold of the top edge of the car and rolled himself onto the roof. He panted and looked at the goat. "Thanks," he said. The goat cooed this time, nudging Bobert's head with its own, thankfully avoiding poking him in the eye with one of its horns, and then it flew off into the night.

Bobert rolled over and started to crawl toward the middle of the car, where the diagrams Shmebecca had shown them said the vent would be. The train was swaying side to side, and even though Bobert felt very unsteady and more than a little scared, he was glad that he wasn't dangling from a rope anymore.

He tried to crawl as quietly as possible. He wished he knew

how the others were doing. There hadn't been any screaming or other commotion coming from the train, which felt like a good sign. Hopefully everyone had boarded okay.

Approaching the vent, Bobert reached into his pocket for the screwdriver he'd put there. It was hard to do while wearing the rope harness, but he still needed the harness to lower himself safely inside the car, so he had to shimmy his hand into the pocket until his fingers just barely hooked onto the cool metal.

Before he started unscrewing the vent, he peered through the little slats to get a glimpse at what might be waiting for him in there. The room below was well lit, though he couldn't tell where the light was coming from. Maneuvering around to get a view from as many angles as he could, he gathered that there wasn't anyone in there, at least not that he could see. He breathed a sigh of relief and got to work.

18

CANDELABRA JUMPED ONTO THE BACK OF THE TRAIN, proud of how smoothly everything had gone. Even knowing what she knew about how the night would go, she did take pride in her ability to accomplish things, to contribute to this plan. She would use her skills again in the future, use that drive she had to do the right thing. Although, she reminded herself, she was using those skills tonight too. Even if not everyone would see it that way.

For now she didn't want to think about any of that, though. She had to see the plan through. For Sandraliere. For things to change for good.

She turned around and saw the ugly, painful fall that was waiting for her if she slipped. She hooked her left arm and leg around the ladder attached to the train (Why was it there? Who knew?), then leaned forward, reaching out with her free arm to the open back door.

She took a few sharp breaths, gearing herself up. Then, when she felt ready, she launched herself into the train car, rolling onto the floor with a thump that made her lose her breath for a moment.

After a few seconds she got to her feet and went to the front of the car. She peeked in through the window leading to the next car. There was a woman in a security uniform facing the window. Candelabra whipped her head back and held her breath, waiting to hear some sort of alarm. When a couple of seconds went by without anything happening, she stole another glance and noticed that the woman's eyes were closed. Even though she was standing up, her head was resting against the wall. She might have been asleep.

Other than the guard, there was a folding chair in the corner, and a glass water bottle. They had guessed as much, but the fact that the car was empty otherwise, with no cargo to speak of, seemed to confirm that the muffin was on board. Not that Candelabra was still wondering if it was there.

She had brought her backpack with her, and inside she had the weighted blanket. She took it out, tucked it under her arm, and slowly turned the train's door handle.

It creaked, but the sound was buried under the noise of the train, so Candelabra had to continue with the plan. She unfurled the blanket, took another couple of steps, and right as Candelabra was going to toss the blanket, a loud crash rang out elsewhere on the train.

The guard's eyes shot open, and she reached for the wand at her belt, which Candelabra was noticing just now. The kids had not been prepared for magical guards at all.

"Hey," the guard said. "What are you—"

Candelabra had briefly hoped that she wouldn't have to follow through with this, but that was snuffed out as soon as the guard spoke. Candelabra heaved the blanket onto the woman just as she was pointing her wand.

A bolt of lightning shot out from the wand, but it came just as the blanket enveloped the guard, so it singed a black streak onto the metal floor. The woman was trapped beneath it, wriggling beneath the incredible weight of the blanket. "Why am I so comfortable!" she shouted at Candelabra.

Candelabra covered the guard's mouth with her hand, making a face as the woman kept screaming into it. "Ew, her spit is all over my hand," she said, even though there was no one around. She wondered if she should assure the guard somehow. If the guard maybe even knew what was happening and that all of this was unnecessary. But no. No one from outside could communicate with the train. That was why they'd told her to keep on with the plan.

She could tell that the guard was already losing some of her fight. Within a few seconds, her eyelids started to flutter.

Once the guard was snoring, Candelabra stood and waited by the door, making sure no one else had heard the commotion. When she couldn't hear anything, Candelabra slid it open to go to the next car. The noise of the train roaring through the night got much louder, which helped explain why no one had come to investigate the guard's shouting. But it meant that whatever crash had startled the guard from her standing sleep had been really loud. Candelabra hoped that no one had been hurt. Whatever she was about to be responsible for, her intentions were not to cause any harm.

Passing through the rickety space between the two cars, she was glad that there was a window into the next one, and that that car seemed to be empty. Well, except for the chickens. There were about thirty of them, but they were seated casually in tiny seats designed for them. Candelabra had forgotten that chickens weren't farm animals in Joviala. They weren't exactly equal citizens—the seats they were in did *not* look comfortable at all, and there was clearly no food-and-beverage service on this train—but they weren't food, either.

Candelabra slid the door open, waving and grimace-smiling as all the chickens tilted their heads quizzically at her and started clucking. "Just passing through," she said, avoiding stepping on them. "Don't mind me."

THE GREATEST HEIST IN JOVIALA

She had one more car to cross, and then she'd be at the fifth car, where the muffin was. Candelabra hoped dearly that Bobert had made it in there all right, and that when she knocked the secret knock, he would slide the door open with that big, goofy grin of his. Even if he would lose it shortly after.

19

SHMEBECCA HAD ALMOST MISSED THE TRAIN. AFTER tossing the fake rat-bird into the bushes beside the tracks, she and Jennizabeth had scrambled to catch up to the accelerating vehicle. She'd managed to boost Jennizabeth onto the steps of the third car, but then it had started speeding up even more.

Shmebecca hadn't run in a very long time, and she'd regretted that fact as she saw Jennizabeth pulling away from her, and when she couldn't make her legs move fast enough to catch up. She groaned, wondering who had time to become both an expert on local mountains *and* a fast runner.

"Get on the next car!" Jennizabeth yelled. Which had been a good idea, because the steps were just about to come up on Shmebecca, so she was able to quickly react and grab the handlebar. For a second she lost her footing, and she was sure she was going to get pulled under the train wheels. And despite believing that she would do anything for her mountain, she did have the thought: *Well, this is a stupid way to go.*

THE GREATEST HEIST IN JOVIALA

But her grip held, and even though her feet dragged briefly on the ground, she didn't suffer anything but some scuffed shoes and a scraped shin. She pulled herself onto the train, huffing and surprisingly close to tears. But she didn't have the time for that.

Then she discovered that the door into the train was locked. She pulled on it and was about to knock frantically when she remembered that there were people inside who wouldn't be very happy with a kid showing up unannounced on the train they were trying to protect.

She'd anticipated a locked door, though, and reached into her pocket for the master key she'd found in a cereal box. (People assume that kingdoms with magic don't have cereal, for some reason. Lands everywhere have cereal.) It had proven to be surprisingly effective. She'd once used it when she'd gotten herself locked out when no one else was home, and once to get into the science lab at school in order to grab a spectrometer.

She tried to get a look through the window at the inside of the car, but the door faced a bathroom, which was currently unoccupied. There was no chance that she'd be able to hear anything happening inside, so she started looking for the keyhole.

The problem became apparent quickly. Even the world's best master key couldn't work on a door with no keyhole.

Forgetting her caution, she banged on the door in frustration. Now what?

Now this: Stanbert's head appeared in the window, no longer wearing his homemade sock-mask. She couldn't hear him, but she could read his lips when he furrowed his brow and asked, "What are you doing out there?"

"Open the door!" she said, exaggerating her lip movements.

Stanbert cupped a hand to his ear, doing the classic sign for *I can't hear you.*

Shmebecca banged on the door and gestured frantically to it, after which Stanbert nodded in understanding and a few seconds later slid it open. She rushed inside, looking past him to take in what was going on.

"Nice to see you, too," Stanbert grumbled.

"Is everything going according to plan?" she asked, right as she caught sight of the two guards rolling around on the floor. Both had socks stuffed in their mouths, muffling their shouts.

One was handcuffed to his own ankles, which Shmebecca was pretty impressed by. "How'd you manage that?"

"Well, I tied his shoelaces together, and when he reached down, I slapped the handcuffs on."

"And her?" Shmebecca pointed at the other one.

"She was laughing so hard at him that she fell over by herself, and it was pretty easy to tie her up with the spare shoelaces you gave me," Stanbert said. "I'm pretty good at this heist stuff. Maybe I should become a professional thief."

"We can talk about that later," she said. "Any sign of the others?"

Just then the door leading to the front of the train opened up, and Jennizabeth walked through. She took in the scene and smiled. "Nice. This is turning out easier than I thought it would. Thanks for doing all the hard stuff," she said to Stanbert.

"Let's not get too excited," Shmebecca said, moving down the car and double-checking that the guards were securely tied up. "We haven't accomplished anything until we have the muffin and it's hidden somewhere the Fun Corporation can never find it."

The three of them continued through the train car, which was empty except for the guards on the floor, a water cooler in the corner, and a sign on the wall that read: IT'S BEEN 3,000 DAYS SINCE OUR LAST ACCIDENT!

"Does this count as an accident?" Stanbert asked.

Neither of the girls answered as a loud crash sounded from up ahead. It was hard to tell exactly what the noise was, but hopefully it was one of the other members of their crew executing the plan. There was another clatter, the sound of wood absorbing some thud, and a grunt. Shmebecca and Jennizabeth exchanged looks, and Shmebecca felt panic closing in on her chest. The mountain had saved her; she couldn't fail it. She couldn't let it be maimed or destroyed, all those eons of history and geology eradicated to make way for a stupid amusement park. Even if no one else cared about it. *Especially* because no one else cared about it.

Whatever was happening in the other car had better be according to plan. They moved ahead, and soon they were in between cars three and four.

Shmebecca was eager to neutralize the rest of the guards and get to the muffin. Every moment she wasn't in front of it was another moment when the whole operation could be falling apart. Still, she stepped gingerly out onto the platform just beyond the door. The wind was roaring, and the metal wheels screeched on the tracks below. The cars jostled every few moments, and it was like everything inside them was being shaken by a giant toddler. Whereas inside the cars had felt safe, out here it felt like at any moment whatever was connecting the cars to each other would come loose, and she'd be tossed into the treacherous depths below. Well, maybe not depths. If there were depths, maybe she could land softly. The treacherous shallows below.

Gripping whatever she could, trying not to look down at the ground whipping past beneath her feet, she stepped across the chasm and onto the next platform, making sure to stay out of sight of the window to the next car. Once Stanbert and

THE GREATEST HEIST IN JOVIALA

Jennizabeth were beside her, she poked her head into view.

"Nuts," she said, dipping back out of sight.

"What?" Stanbert responded, trying to catch a glimpse of what was in the next car. Shmebecca would have tried to stop him, except all the guards she saw were facing the other way. That wasn't the problem. The problem was that there were five in that one room, when there should have only been three more in the whole train.

"That's okay," Shmebecca said, mostly to herself. "We've got plenty of sleeping potions."

"Um, I know I was just saying I'm a heist expert, but I don't think I can knock out five security people at once. Maybe two?" Stanbert shoved his hands in his pockets. "Man, maybe I'm terrible at heists. I should retire." He kicked the wall. "That's settled. This is my last job. One last hurrah."

Shmebecca shushed him. "Let me think." She swung her backpack off one shoulder and unzipped it. "What other supplies do we have left?" She pulled out the sleep potion she had in three different forms: There was the powder, which they could throw at the guards, but they had to be careful not to breathe any in themselves. Then there was the water balloon full of it, which could maybe knock out one or two of them—all five if they had their mouths open at the same time and enough drops made their way into each mouth, Shmebecca supposed. The last form was a pillow that had been compressed. If you pulled the string to turn it into a full-sized pillow, then hit someone with the pillow, they would have a very nice eight hours of sleep.

"Neither of you has the hugging snakes?" Jennizabeth asked. "I just have this lollipop, which I don't think will help." Jennizabeth sniffed it for some reason, then tucked it back into her pocket.

"Darn, no—Shmayden has the snakes. Stanbert, do you have anything?" Shmebecca looked in through the window again. It seemed like the guards were trying to get into the next car. Which was where Bobert and the muffin were. "They must have heard him in there. We should hurry." She handed Stanbert the pillow and Jennizabeth the water balloon. Then she pulled out the sweater she'd brought in case it got chilly and started tying it like a bandana around her face. "You two go for the three on the right. I'll blow the powder on the two on the left. Cover your faces too. Or hold your breath."

"For how long?" Jennizabeth asked, worry in her voice.

That was a detail Shmebecca didn't have time to think about. They had to get inside before the guards got to Bobert, or before one of them thought to tell the engineer to stop the train or send a signal for more guards or something. The only way this plan would work was right now, on the train, while as few people as possible were aware it was happening.

"Ready?" Shmebecca asked. She waited for the two

Nefarians to nod in understanding, and then she slid the door open.

As she rushed into the fourth car, Shmebecca started yelling. She didn't know why. It just felt like the right thing to do. She had the powder in a little sachet, and she pulled it loose, aiming it at the two guards who were trying to pull open the door to the next car, probably confused as to why there was a child screaming her head off.

This yelling caused the guards to yell too, at first out of surprise, and then because when someone is yelling at the top of their lungs for no apparent reason, the typical human reaction is to yell back. Stanbert and Jennizabeth joined in on the yelling, following Shmebecca's lead. If someone had stopped them and asked them why, and if they were being honest, they would have said that they were feeling overwhelmed by everything that was going on and yelling seemed to help.

Throughout all this yelling—during which Stanbert made pillow contact with one of the guards, knocking him out instantly—no one noticed that the door to the muffin car had slid open. Shmebecca herself was too busy trying to shake the sleep potion powder out. Except that it mostly just fell to the floor instead of puffing out in a cloud of dust like she'd expected. She realized that was probably a safety feature to keep the user from knocking themselves out.

The two guards she'd approached watched as the powder

she tried to shake at them fell uselessly to the floor. One of them smirked and took a step toward her. Shmebecca wondered if it was safe to reach inside the sachet and toss a handful straight into the security woman's face.

Before she could decide, the security woman seemed to grow a full foot.

Except, no, that wasn't right. She was higher up, not taller.

And it was because someone had grabbed her from beneath the armpits and raised her off the floor. She was now kicking her feet wildly, like a toddler trying to learn how to walk. But she wasn't going anywhere. At least not of her own volition.

Shmebecca watched as the guard was thrown against the wall. Where the woman had been standing before, Shmebecca now saw another woman, decked out in warrior gear from some other land (Jovialese warrior gear was notoriously sparse, so she knew it wasn't that).

"Miss Petunias?" Shmebecca asked, wondering what the Nefarian chaperone was doing here.

As a response, Miss Petunias grabbed the sachet from Shmebecca's hands, formed it into a small funnel, and poured a little bit directly into the guard's mouth. The guard started snoring immediately, but Miss Petunias was already onto the next guard, who was about to run into the muffin room. She grabbed him by the collar of his shirt, pulled him backward, and in one fluid motion poured more powder onto his face, turning away to avoid any puffing up into her own nose.

Shmebecca watched in awe but knew that there were still three other guards to deal with. She looked at the other side of the room and saw that Jennizabeth was being held by the biggest guard as a shield to protect himself from Stanbert, who was aiming the pillow at him. He was doing this while trying to avoid the last two guards, who were closing in on him, apparently unaware of the other people in the room.

Shmebecca looked at the door that had slid open, realizing that she also wasn't fully aware of the other people there with her. She saw that Bobert, Shmelix, Shmayden, and Candelabra were all staring back at her, all wearing the same stupefied and thrilled expression on their faces. At some point the yelling had stopped, but Shmebecca couldn't say for sure when that had happened. Nor when, exactly, all her fellow heisters had arrived.

Now Miss Petunias took two long strides and jumped in the air, seemingly moving in slow motion. Which totally solidified the fact that she was a warrior of some sort. Only people who'd been in fight scenes could move in slow motion.

Her right knee landed on one of the guards closing in on Stanbert, hitting him in his lower back. In almost the same motion, she rolled and used her left heel to kick the other guard in the face. Spit spewed across the room, and at least three of the kids yelled in disgust.

The guard who'd been holding Jennizabeth suddenly realized that maybe he should focus on the one adult in the room who was kicking everyone's butts (and faces). Before he could decide how to go about doing that, though, Miss Petunias grabbed the pillow from Stanbert, whacked the guard in the face, and then caught his head and gently laid him down on the train floor.

She clapped her hands together, tied the sleeping-potion sachet tight, and tossed it to Shmebecca. Then she looked at the children. "Anyone care to explain what we're doing here, then?"

20

After Bobert had finished unscrewing the vent to lower himself into the muffin car, he'd forgotten to toss the vent cover over the side of the train or leave it anywhere else but dangling on the edge of the vent. So, when he kicked his feet around to begin his descent, he kicked the vent cover, sending it crashing down directly on top of the muffin.

"Oops," he said aloud to no one. He stared down at the room, expecting someone to come running in. But no one did. Either the guards were locked out themselves, or no one had heard the crash. It was fortunate that the aquarium with the electric piranhas hadn't broken, even if the glass case holding the muffin wouldn't.

Then he realized it was probably smart to get inside the train instead of waiting for someone to catch him and prevent him from lowering himself safely into the car. He could think about all the whys later.

After testing that the grappling hook was still safely in

place (if he ever found that goat again, he'd have to give it a treat), he eased himself down, grimacing at the pressure the rope exerted on his legs.

When he landed inside, he untied the rope harness and took a moment to admire the muffin. Even through the glass case and water tank it was submerged in, with all the piranhas swimming about, the muffin shone a beautiful golden color that seemed to glow. Actually, it seemed to be the only source of light in the room. Cool. Bobert wondered if eating it would cause your insides to glow. The blueberries, too, gave off a pretty blue light. He couldn't help but want Candelabra there with him to see it. He reminded himself that she was still on the train, and that they'd get to bask in the defeat of an evil scheme together. Just because she wasn't there at that exact moment didn't mean she wasn't with him, even though that was what it felt like. It only felt that way because she'd been a little weird before. That had probably just been nerves. After all, last time he'd only seen her when she was rescuing him, not before she came to Matt's castle.

That was when he heard the shouting coming from both sides of the train. There was the sound of loud footsteps as, he assumed, guards ran toward the muffin to protect it. Hoping his friends would reach him first, he listened at the door for the secret knock they'd come up with. The group had argued for a long time about what it would be, everyone pitching a different rhythm before falling into a communal drumming session on every nearby surface, until the librarian came over to yell at them to keep it down.

There were a lot of banging sounds on the other side of the door, and what sounded like a lot of chickens clucking up a storm, but not the two short knocks, followed by three long ones, followed by six medium knocks that they'd agreed on.

So Bobert examined the muffin's enclosure for any safeguards they hadn't known about. The piranhas eyed him suspiciously through the glass, and though they looked grumpy, he wouldn't have assumed they were bitier than any other fish. The bolts of electricity that zapped through the water every few seconds were more intimidating.

While the shouting and clanging continued outside, Bobert discovered a little red button just below the stone structure that held the water tank and the muffin. As he was weighing whether to press it, he heard the secret knock coming from the back door.

Bobert rushed over and unlocked the three deadbolts. When the door slid open, he saw Shmelix and Candelabra looking back at him, covered in chicken feathers.

"Um," he said. He couldn't quite wrap his mind around what he was seeing. He made eye contact with Candelabra, waiting for an explanation, but she quickly looked away, embarrassed.

"Don't ask!" Shmelix yelled before Bobert could say anything else. "I'm covered in bird fluids *and* other fluids. I'm very angry."

He stormed in, picking at the feathers on his shoulders, before reaching up to the piranha tank, sliding the lid off, and without a second's hesitation dipping a cupped hand in. He splashed the water on his face and then rubbed his hands together. When he was done, he looked up, only then noticing that Bobert and Candelabra were staring at him. "What?" he asked. "I needed to wash up a little."

Bobert stared wide-eyed at the piranhas, one of which was currently buzzing with bright blue sparks.

Shmelix followed his gaze; then, realizing what he'd done, he blinked slowly at the fish tank. One piranha snarled, which Bobert had not known was a thing fish could do. "Well, that could have gone a lot worse," Shmelix said.

That was when the yelling started in the other car, and when Imogene Petunias fell from the sky and into the train car with them. She landed with a softer thud than should have been possible.

Before anyone could ask her where she had come from, how she had found them, or what she was doing there, she ran toward the door leading to the front of the train. She made quick work of the deadbolts, then tossed the door open, leaping across the space between the cars before unleashing mayhem on the guards trying to take down Shmebecca, Stanbert, and Jennizabeth.

After all the fighting was done and they'd explained everything to Miss Petunias, Bobert held his breath, wondering how angry she was going to be at them. Not only were they sneaking out of their host families' homes in the middle of the night to do something very dangerous, but they were also meddling in the affairs of a foreign kingdom. They were breaking laws, and even if Joviala wouldn't punish them like Shmebecca had said, they were probably breaking *some* sort of rule. At the very least some school-exchange rules. In Bobert's defense, it wasn't in the student handbook that they *couldn't* form a crew using their assorted skills to try to steal a magical artifact in order to stop an evil scheme. He wasn't sure if that was a winning defense, though.

He was thankful that Miss Petunias had stepped in to save them, even if he was scared about what she was going to say next. He looked over at Candelabra, certain that she was getting ready to convince their chaperone that they were doing the right thing.

But Candy was just looking down at the floor, chewing on her lip, her arms crossed over her chest.

Shmebecca was the one with her chin raised up and her chest puffed out, as if daring Miss Petunias to try to sabotage her plan.

Except it didn't seem like that was what Miss Petunias was thinking at all. "Okay," she said calmly. "Let's see how we can get this muffin off this train, then."

The train kept rumbling along, the engineer unaware of the shenanigans going on behind him. Candelabra wondered if that was good or bad. She thought about trying to sneak up and talk to him, but she couldn't think of how to do that. Plus, she'd been told to let the plan continue and the train travel all the way to the site. She would just have to wait and see what happened. To just be quiet in the corner.

Thankfully, everyone was very busy trying to figure out how to get to the muffin. Miss Petunias's best guess for the red button that Bobert had discovered was that it was part of a weight sensor on the stone pedestal. If they tried to remove the piranha tank, either the driver would be alerted, or—and this was Miss Petunias's guess—some other security measure would trap them inside the car until every invested authority in the many kingdoms came to deal with them. The muffin was so powerful that *a lot* of authorities were invested.

Plus, there would be a curse to contend with. Whatever that would be.

"Wait, can we go back to the 'every invested authority' bit?" Stanbert said.

Candelabra tried to swallow the taste of guilt rising up her

THE GREATEST HEIST IN JOVIALA

throat. She felt hot and cold at the same time, and she stepped slowly away from the conversation, toward the door that led to the next car, desperate for fresh air.

"Well, yes," Miss Petunias said in a tone that was somewhere between patient and patronizing. "You do know that if you get caught there'll be consequences, right?"

All the kids turned to look at Shmebecca, and Candelabra was happy for their attention being diverted so she could back up more.

"We're not gonna get caught," Shmebecca said, more resolute than she'd been before. "Everything's going fine."

Candelabra creaked the door open, and thankfully, even though there was an immediate roar of wind when she did, no one turned in her direction.

Imogene Petunias sighed. "Seems like you're the leader of this little operation. Which I respect. But if you're bringing others into the fire with you, you have to let them know how much they can expect to get burned, you understand?"

"That makes it sound scarier than what I was ready for," Jennizabeth said.

"Is there more that we should know?" Shmayden said to Shmebecca. "Or more that *they* have to know?"

"Maybe—I don't know!" Shmebecca said. "Let's just finish this plan and we don't have to worry about it, right? How do we get to the muffin without alerting anyone?"

That was enough for Candelabra. She stepped out into the space between the cars for some fresh air. She thought about her sister back home, thought about what it would be like to actually hug her, to be in the same room with her, not separated by a painting, a curse, a whole world. She couldn't wait for that to be the case. She'd been waiting so long for that bit of her life to change that she couldn't believe that she was closer than she'd ever been since Sandraliere got trapped in her painting. It still felt so far away from happening.

In the roaring dark beyond the train, she could make out the trees whipping past beneath the moonlight, the imposing silhouette of Mount Saint Helenhunt getting closer. There were artificial lights at its base: the construction equipment awaiting the crews in the morning, probably. Candelabra couldn't help but picture Mr. Eyebrows there waiting for her and her friends. She tried not to think about what authorities might be waiting there too. About the long list of charges that would be read to them. Just to them.

"Brainstorming?" Bobert asked from behind her, yelling a little to be heard over the train's clacking. It seemed he'd followed her.

"Something like that," Candelabra said. She turned to face him, tried to smile to throw off any suspicions he might have. "How's it going in there?"

Bobert turned to look back, scratching his head. "I think

the best idea we have so far is that we try to eat the piranhas. Which I don't think counts as a good idea at all, but I haven't heard a better one."

They both looked back into the train car, where Stanbert and Jennizabeth were playing rock-paper-scissors while Shmelix and Shmayden held their hands over the water tank, practicing a scooping motion. "All these people," Candelabra said, "helping Shmebecca, caring about what she does, all to try to keep things from changing."

"I think it's about more than that," Bobert said. "Although I don't necessarily think that's so wrong. Why would we want anything to change?"

The look in his eyes was so innocent, so hopeful, that she had to look away. She focused instead on the night sky, the stars steady despite how fast everything around them was moving.

"Everything okay?" Bobert asked.

She just laughed, happy that the tear that came to her eye rolled down her cheek on the side Bobert couldn't see. "Yeah, of course. Why?"

"You've just seemed a little . . . off the last few days. And I wanted to make sure."

That made her want to cry even more, but she managed to swallow the emotion threatening to climb up her throat. She pretended to see something interesting on the horizon, turning her head so he couldn't see her. The wind, at least, served as a likely excuse for why her eyes were watery.

"Guys!" Shmebecca called out from inside. "We have a plan."

Shmebecca wasn't sure why Miss Petunias was helping them, but she wasn't about to stop everything and have a whole conversation about it. Especially not when they needed a lot of strength to carry the muffin. Strength that Shmebecca had hoped she'd be able to find some work-around for.

It was clear that without Miss Petunias, though—whose strength was considerably greater than Shmebecca would have expected from a field-trip chaperone—the kids would have had no chance.

Bobert and Candelabra both came back from the space between the train cars, and though Shmebecca wanted to ask what they'd been doing there, there were more pressing matters to deal with. Miss Petunias was studying the perimeter of the glass case, looking very much like someone who'd helped steal stuff in the past. She was squatting in a professional manner, looking at little details of the fish tank that no one would think to look at except for an expert of some sort or another.

"Who are you?" Shmebecca had to ask.

"Just someone who's good at problem-solving," she answered. "Okay, everyone, gather around."

The kids did as they were told, crowding around the fish

tank, looking a mix of nervous, tired, and excited. Shmebecca felt strangely thrilled that she was closest to Miss Petunias, even though just a couple of hours ago she hadn't wanted the woman to know what they were doing at all. Was this possible? Adults who listened to what a kid said was important, and were willing to put themselves at risk for it?

"So the glass container with the muffin is unbreakable. But we don't need to break it at all, right? We don't need the muffin; we just need it out of their hands."

"Except . . . piranhas," Shmelix said, pointing at the two dozen or so fish in the bathtub-sized tank. "Also, wasn't there a curse involved?"

"Rumored, yeah," Shmebecca said.

"Well, here's the thing," Miss Petunias said. "We don't have to go through the water and the fish to get to the muffin. That'd be the quicker way, but not the smarter way."

"What other way is there? They're between us and the muffin," Stanbert said slowly, like he was explaining something very basic to a not-very-smart person.

Miss Petunias smiled, like she'd expected this. She tapped Shmebecca's shoulder, where her backpack was still strapped to her. "Can I borrow this?" she asked. Shmebecca nodded eagerly, slipping the backpack off and handing it over, not even caring when Miss Petunias turned it upside down, emptying its remaining contents on the floor.

Shmebecca watched her round pencil case roll to the edge of the train car, then back toward her feet as the train took a bend around the mountain. They must have been getting close to the construction site, but Shmebecca tamped down the worry.

Miss Petunias held the empty backpack over the tank; then, making sure her hands didn't come into contact with the water, she scooped out a whole backpack full of it. A few sparks shot out of the piranhas she'd captured, but it seemed like the backpack's vinyl lining was keeping the electricity from shocking Miss Petunias.

"I don't think we have enough backpacks to empty all the water out," Shmayden said.

"And what do we do with the piranhas? I know they're mean, but we're not just gonna kill them, are we?" Jennizabeth asked, crouching down to look at one of the fish, which was particularly ugly, and looked like it had about sixty teeth too many.

Shmebecca had a thought, and she ran over to the space between the cars to confirm what she'd suspected. "We're passing the Wiggly-Shmiggly River!" she said, jogging back to the group. "It's where the piranhas come from anyway. The tracks run right alongside it. We can toss them in from here, and they'll probably be happier. But we have to hurry. We're only a few miles away from the construction site."

THE GREATEST HEIST IN JOVIALA

Some of the kids cheered, though a few of them looked wary about sticking any part of their hands near the tank. They didn't have much time to be uncertain, though. Miss Petunias handed the backpack to Shmebecca and clapped her hands twice. "What are we waiting for! You heard the girl, let's get these fish in the river. Everyone with a bag, start scooping. Watch your fingers!"

The next few minutes were a flurry of activity. Shmebecca herself was focused only on her backpack, scooping out as many of the fish as quickly as possible. It was a thrill to watch them disappear from the large tank, to watch the muffin emerge from the water. Every now and then someone would shout "Ow!" as they got zapped, but no one got bitten. A few times Shmebecca met Bobert's eyes and mouthed a thank-you to him. He smiled his sweet, dopey grin and continued helping.

Just as they were getting to the last fish, the whole train jolted. Candelabra and Shmelix collided into each other, and Stanbert went sprawling on the floor, thankfully not getting seriously hurt, or flying out of the train.

"What's happening?" Jennizabeth asked. The jolt had caused her to drop the tote bag she was using, and one of the piranhas was now flopping around on the floor. She tried to scoop it back up while telling it that everything was going to be all right.

"We're stopping," Miss Petunias said. "They're either onto

us, or we're about to arrive at the construction site. Which means we have to pull this muffin out right now if we want it out of their hands."

"What about the weight sensor? Won't it lock us in as soon as we grab the muffin?" Shmelix asked, tugging at his earlobe, something he did when he was nervous.

Miss Petunias rubbed her chin, thinking. She maneuvered around to the other side of the tank, where the red button was, and examined it for a few tense moments. A squeal rang out, which Shmebecca recognized as the train's braking system. She looked back at the team she'd assembled, wanting to impart a sense of confidence in them. They could finish this. They could make this happen. Save her mountain. Save the kingdom. And most of them looked like they believed already.

"One second," Miss Petunias said, raising a finger. She trotted into the other car, then reappeared carrying one of the sleeping guards she'd helped knock out with the powder. Everyone parted, raising eyebrows as they watched her lift him over her head and then set him down gently in the tank, on his side. The glass container with the muffin pressed against his lower back, and there were still a few inches of water left in the tank, but he didn't stir at all.

"Okay, everyone climb into the tank," Miss Petunias said.

Bobert started pulling himself onto the pedestal immediately, though the others looked a little less sure—like maybe they should ask a few questions first. After a few moments, Stanbert plopped down and unlaced his shoes, saying they were new and that he wasn't going to get them wet and covered in piranha poop. Which almost sidetracked them into a conversation about whether or not piranha poop was visible in the water, but Shmebecca derailed them.

"Why didn't the weight sensor go off with the extra weight?" she asked.

"I've seen these before," Miss Petunias said. "These only go off if there's less weight than when they're set, not more. So what we have to do is all of us get on the pedestal. I'll try to lift the muffin myself, and you guys help from below. Once I have it up high enough, I'll get off the pedestal and shuffle my way off the train." She looked at the fish tank and made a thinking noise. "Wait, maybe we need a couple more guards in there, just in case." She left and came back carrying a dozing guard over each shoulder, and she arranged them in the tub. "That should do it."

The train jolted again and let out a horn blast. "We need to hurry!" Shmebecca shouted. Now all the kids started scrambling to get in the tub, following Miss Petunias's instructions.

Then a voice came from somewhere ahead on the train. "Hey! What's going on here?"

Shmebecca recognized it as the train engineer's voice. "Oh no," she cried. "What are we going to do?"

"I'll take care of it," Candelabra said. She was the only one who hadn't climbed on the pedestal yet. Come to think of it, she was the only one who looked like she didn't think they were going to succeed. She'd been hovering near the end of the car by the door, glancing solemnly out the window.

Shmebecca watched as Candelabra turned toward the front of the train. Before she left their car, she looked back, meeting Shmebecca's eyes. Shmebecca nodded, but Candelabra didn't return the nod. It almost looked like she was about to cry. But then Miss Petunias was squatting down beside her, shouting for everyone to get ready.

When she looked back over, Candelabra was gone. Off to use her talking-to-adults skills to buy time with the engineer. But why was doubt starting to creep into Shmebecca's stomach and tickle up and down her spine? Was doubt even allowed to be in two places at once like that?

There it was anyway: the thought that they would never be able to do this. That they were too close to the construction site, too close to getting caught, and they still had to do the hardest part of the whole operation: lift the muffin and get away with it. Lifting it needed the strength of ten warriors, and there wasn't a single one among them. Okay, maybe Miss Petunias was one, though it was hard to think of her as a warrior and not a teacher, despite what she'd done to those guards. Which was cool, but would she be enough?

When Shmebecca had been stuck facedown in the hot mud,

the mountain had found the strength within it to burp her to safety. And now when it needed her the most, she was going to come up short. She was going to get Candelabra and the other Nefarians in serious trouble, and all for nothing. All because she wasn't a normal Jovialese kid who could just be happy with the pleasant side of everything. She had to get obsessed with a mountain, and want to know everything about it, care about it in a way that wasn't normal.

"Shmebecca, we need you!" someone called out.

Shmebecca snapped back to the present, realizing she was the only one within reach of the muffin who wasn't squatting trying to lift it. She matched everyone's position, trying to find space for her fingers on the smooth glass. Shmayden was grunting near her, and she could see the muscles on Miss Petunias's forearms tensing, but it all felt so useless all of a sudden. "We're gonna fail," she blurted out. "This was a bad idea; this is too hard. I can't even hold on to the stupid thing."

She still had a hand on the muffin case, which made it easy for her to sense that it hadn't budged at all. "We're not strong enough." She was blubbering now, tears bursting through the brave front she'd tried to put up. In other situations she might have felt embarrassed. But in a few days she'd never see most of these kids again, Shmayden and Shmelix had seen her cry enough, and there were plenty more important things going on.

"Of course we are," Bobert said. He pulled his hands away

from the muffin case and put them on her shoulders, turning her so that she would face him completely. Beyond him she could see that the sky wasn't pitch black anymore. It was that soft purple of an incoming dawn, and in that light she could see that the train was moving very slowly now.

"It takes ten warriors," she said. "There's not a single one here. Or, maybe *just* one," she added, shooting a look at Miss Petunias.

"Are you kidding?" he said. "You've led us on a mission to stop a mountain from being moved. We've jumped aboard a speeding train, taken down more security guards than we planned on, and are moments away from gathering our strength to steal one of the most powerful magical artifacts known to man! All to save Joviala from destruction. We *are* warriors, every one of us. And you most of all."

For a brief moment everything else fell away. The train's gentle rocking and loud clacking, her exhaustion, her worry, the strange place she was in: a mostly emptied fish tank, with seven other people, on top of three snoring security guards, near a magical muffin that could destroy her mountain or save it with its absence. She thought about the fact that her mountain might not be there tomorrow. And who knew what it would be replaced by. Chaos of one sort or another. Then an amusement park, if anything survived. Nothing would be as it was. Nothing would be as it should.

THE GREATEST HEIST IN JOVIALA

For now, though, there was just her and Bobert. His words filling her up. Maybe it was silly. Maybe it was just her wanting to believe so badly that they *could* that she would have latched onto any slight words of hope. Whatever the reason, she believed him.

No. That wasn't exactly right.

There was nothing to believe or not believe. He was simply right. She was a warrior. They *all* were.

"Loving this moment you're having," Shmayden called out, her voice straining. "But I just felt this thing move, and it'd be great to have four more hands here."

"It moved again!" Stanbert called out.

"Yeah, I felt it!" Shmelix joined in. "Get your butts in here!"

Shmebecca and Bobert looked at each other and both laughed (Shmebecca had to wipe some snot away as she did so). Then they retook their positions next to the others.

"On three!" Bobert yelled. "One—"

"We don't have time for counting," Shmebecca cut in. "Lift!"

No one needed to be told again. There was a collective groan as they tried to find a handle on the glass cube and move it. At first it was like trying to move the train itself. It was incredible how heavy such a small object could be.

Then she felt it give way. It lifted enough that she could get the tips of her fingers under it.

It felt like she was on her mountain for a second. Like she'd been digging for a particular piece of agate. Something big for her mosaic, buried in the dirt. And now she was searching for the edge. It always felt like the ground was hanging on desperately to each rock she dug for. Like it would only come loose for her when she'd earned it, when she'd found the full shape of it and reverently dug away the rest.

Thankfully, the people of Joviala have very strong fingers.

21

THEY WERE DOING IT! THEY WERE LIFTING THE MUFFIN OF Glory. As he helped raise the muffin, Bobert slowly went from a full squat to kind of a half one that made a different part of his legs hurt. But he didn't care. They were raising the muffin by at least a foot or two. Just in time, it seemed, because the train's brakes started to squeal.

The muffin was above Miss Petunias's knees now, almost past Bobert's hips. He maneuvered himself under it so he could lift with his shoulders. He wished his parents could see this. He wished Candelabra could see it. Where was she? It seemed that whatever it was she'd said to the engineer had worked for a time. He was sure she'd come running back in a second to help.

Although maybe they wouldn't need her help anymore. Bobert could feel the momentum building, and the muffin was getting higher and higher, almost as if by magic. Except it wasn't magic. It was all of them coming together to help Shmebecca save her kingdom.

Miss Petunias gave out one last grunt of effort, and then she shouted, "Okay, everyone move! I need room to climb out." She strained with the weight, but as Bobert stepped away, he saw that she mostly had it under control. One day he was going to have to ask her why she was so strong.

But now he just made sure that she had a way to get off the train. He hopped out and helped Jennizabeth down. As the train's brakes squealed again, the kids, all sweaty now, moved out of the way, shaking out their wrists and looking up at the sight of a red-faced Imogene Petunias standing knee-high in the fish tank.

"Will you be able to get out?" Shmebecca asked, a bit of the worry returning to her voice.

Without bothering to respond, Miss Petunias placed one foot on the edge of the fish tank and shifted her body weight forward. Even with the guards sleeping at the bottom, the fish tank tipped toward the floor, thanks to the weight of the muffin.

"Step back!" Bobert said, realizing what she was doing—and that Miss Petunias needed to conserve her strength. Everyone scrambled to the other side as she tried again to tip the fish tank. It tilted slightly forward, but then the guards' weight rolling around balanced it back down.

They were all just watching until Jennizabeth yelled at them to push on Miss Petunias's next attempt. "It'll help tip it over!"

They lined up again, hands flat on the side of the fish tank.

Bobert's muscles were already sore from the effort of lifting the muffin, but that was something he could worry about later. For now, the adrenaline pumping through his veins made it seem like the pain couldn't touch him. Next to him, Shmebecca was straining so loudly she sounded almost like a teakettle ready to boil. Her arms were shaking as she pushed, and it made Bobert want to try even harder. He dug a little deeper so he would know that he had pushed as hard as he possibly could have.

After three communal pushes, he felt the tank finally tipping over. He worried that with her hands taken up by the muffin, Miss Petunias would fall flat on her face. But she kept her foot on top of the fish tank and rode it down like she was surfing. Before it could hit the pedestal and shatter she hopped out, landing with her knees bent. Two of the guards rolled out onto the floor, still snoring. Thankfully, as the aquarium exploded into thousands of little pieces, neither one seemed to have been cut by the glass. One guard was left on the pedestal, arms hanging over the edge.

Now there was one more jolt as the train came to a full stop. It was suddenly very quiet. Quiet enough that Bobert could hear voices. As the others helped Miss Petunias up from her squat, Bobert ran over to the space between the cars and looked out.

Bobert recognized the scenery immediately, even without all the equipment and people in hard hats (and other kinds of hats, too). But there were some workers there, and a few were walking toward the train, holding hand torches.

Bobert bolted back to the train car and told everyone what he had seen. "We'll do what Candelabra did with the engineer and stall them," he suggested. "We'll distract them while Miss Petunias escapes from the back."

"Good idea," Shmebecca said. "If you hear them get close, the river is about fifty yards beyond the trees to the west. Just drop it in the river. It's the deepest one in Joviala, has the strongest current, and is so full of flying-goat poop that scientists have trouble studying it. They'll never find the muffin there."

Imogene knew better than to waste any more time. She nodded and then waddled toward the back train car. "I'll . . . leave . . . this way," she huffed.

"What about the curse?" Bobert asked. "Do you feel anything?"

Imogene shrugged, already walking away. "Wouldn't be my first time," she called over her shoulder. "Buy me a few minutes, but keep yourselves out of trouble."

"Okay," Bobert said, looking at the other kids. "What's our strategy here? Run out screaming in all different directions? Ask them where the bathroom is?"

"Act like nothing is wrong and just say hi," Shmelix said. "Remember, this is Joviala. People don't assume evil schemes are underway, not even from a bunch of kids getting off a train they're not supposed to be on at five in the morning or whatever time it is."

"Will that buy Miss Petunias enough time, though?" Jennizabeth asked.

"Just ask them a bunch of questions," Stanbert suggested. "Most adults have no idea what to do when a kid starts talking to them."

"That's true!" Shmayden said. "There's a doorman at our building, and if any of us talk to him, he just starts calling us all 'champ' until we go away."

"Any day now!" Miss Petunias yelled. She was standing by the exit, ready to jump out. The tendons in her neck stood out like they were trying to escape her body, and sweat was pouring down her forehead.

The kids jumped into action and exited the train from the opposite side, chatting nonchalantly and loudly as if it were the most normal thing in the world for them to be there. Bobert let everyone go first, not wanting to leave before finding Candelabra. There was a chance the engineer had gotten suspicious and was apprehending her, and alerting people at the construction site.

"Are you coming?" Shmebecca asked.

"You go ahead. I'm going to look for Candelabra and then I'll join you. Maybe I'll be a secondary distraction if those people keep coming. It'll buy Miss Petunias more time."

"Okay," Shmebecca said, her smile big and easy for the first time all night. "Thanks for everything, Bobert."

"Anytime," he said.

Then she hopped off the train to catch up with the others, who were heading straight toward the construction workers and saying things like "What a fun and normal train ride we were definitely supposed to be on, as scheduled and approved by several adults!"

Bobert headed to the next train car. There was a funny smell there, along with a puddle in a corner and the remnants of some powder, which Bobert assumed was the sleeping potion. He wondered what the guards would make of it all when they woke up, what kind of trouble they would be in for letting the muffin get stolen. He didn't want to get stuck worrying about them, though. They had been part of this evil scheme, or whatever kind of scheme it was, and Bobert much preferred a few people getting in trouble at work than what would happen if they were able to finish their job.

He continued to the next car, peeking outside to see his friends still chattering excitedly. It really felt like they'd done it. Who knew how Miss Petunias had known what they were doing, but now that she had stepped in to help, it felt like the mountain would be saved. She'd toss the muffin in the river, and Mr. Eyebrows would have no choice but to put his amusement park elsewhere.

Bobert was surprised to find the next train car empty. He'd heard Stanbert talking proudly about how he'd slapped the handcuffs on a guard and wrapped up another in shoelaces. He saw some shoelaces on the floor, but no guards. That stopped him for a moment. "Candy?" he asked out loud. But there was no answer. His heart started pounding in his chest, a sense of unease tamping down his momentary urge to celebrate.

He moved on to the last car before the locomotive, more confused than worried. Maybe Candelabra had gotten off the train with the engineer, leading him away from the muffin. That was probably it—she was smart like that.

That made him feel a little better when he entered the locomotive and saw it was empty too.

Bobert stared at the unoccupied engineer's seat. Normally, he would have gone over to it and checked out all the buttons and levers. Instead of relief that she'd made it out safely, though, now a bad feeling was crawling along his skin. He stepped forward, not to explore the train's operating panel but to look out through the window. He hadn't seriously considered the possibility that Candelabra—or any of them for that matter—could get hurt. He hoped that wasn't the case.

Ahead he could see all the diggers, the piles of dirt that they'd already removed from the mountain. There were lights set up, pointing every few feet along the base of the mountain. It was still fairly dark out, but with the coming dawn and those artificial lights, Bobert could see that there was plenty of activity out there. The Fun Corporation hadn't planned on wasting any time. It looked like as soon as they had the muffin, they were going to use it to carry away Mount Saint Helenhunt.

Bobert leaned over to look to his right, and he saw that his friends had met up with the workers who'd been headed toward the train. They were talking and, for the moment, the workers did not seem aware that a heist was underway. He breathed a little sigh of relief, even if there was still a pit forming in his stomach. Where was Candelabra?

He stood there for a moment, thinking, the feeling in his stomach solidifying into full-fledged worry. Where was she? Was she okay? Had she been caught? Hurt?

Not wanting to sit there doing nothing but worrying, he decided he would go check on Miss Petunias. The others had the distraction covered, and she might need some help. Maybe Candelabra had gone around the other side of the train and would be with their chaperone. He rubbed at his fingers, which he just now was realizing were sore from the effort of lifting the muffin.

That was what he was doing as he stepped off the train, only looking up to find his footing. Which was why he didn't notice right away that there were several people standing in a semicircle just in front of the tree line.

He might have kept walking and run into them if it weren't

for Mr. Eyebrows giggling. "The boy is so enthralled with his own fingers! How fascinating!"

Bobert stopped in his tracks. He'd expected to see Miss Petunias shuffling her way through the trees and, yes, perhaps Candelabra at her side.

But he hadn't expected this.

Miss Petunias had almost made it to the tree line. And she was still holding the muffin. But about ten people were blocking her way, and Bobert could tell she was running out of energy, judging by how her arms were shaking, and by the sweat pouring down her temples.

In the middle of those ten people was Mr. Eyebrows, smiling as wide as ever. Bobert recognized a few others from the construction site, including a lady with a hairdo in the shape of a tarantula tap-dancing.

But what held his attention more than anything was Candelabra. She wasn't standing next to Miss Petunias. She wasn't trying to fight Mr. Eyebrows, yelling at these people that they were evil, that they didn't know the damage they were going to cause. She wasn't kicking dirt at Mr. Eyebrows's companions' feet. She wasn't trying to push Miss Petunias deeper into the woods, toward the river.

No, Candelabra was just standing there alongside Mr. Eyebrows. She was facing Miss Petunias and crying. But she didn't look angry. She looked sad.

"I love you Nefarians!" Mr. Eyebrows exclaimed, letting loose another wild giggle. "Things are always interesting when you're around. Isn't that right, Candelabra?"

"What's happening?" Bobert said. He wasn't sure the words even made it across the slight distance between them.

"Oh, it would be my absolute pleasure to explain," Mr. Eyebrows said. "You see, earlier today, I was . . ." He put a hand dramatically to his chin. "Before I explain, maybe we should get the whole crew here so I don't have to repeat myself." He turned to his left, staring down the line of his cronies. Not seeming to find what he was looking for, he turned the other way. "Ah yes, Mr. . . . Train Man," he said, pointing at the engineer. "Let's move the train, have our big reveal." His eyes met Bobert's. "Which you ruined, by the way," he singsonged. "Nothing more fun than a good reveal, but I suppose we'll have to make do."

As the engineer headed back, Miss Petunias groaned loudly and tried running in the opposite direction, through the wall of people. She took barely two steps before running out of breath and stumbling, almost falling face forward in the dirt. She caught herself and pushed onward anyway.

Mr. Eyebrows made a show of sighing. Then he hummed and looked down the line of his allies again before nodding at two large men standing at the end, wearing official-looking capes. They stepped out of line and toward Miss Petunias, then grabbed her, hooking their arms below her armpits.

Now one of the men pulled a pair of gloves out of a pocket in his cape. They were brown leather and looked pretty normal to Bobert. Maybe a little fancy. Then the man reached over and simply snatched the muffin case from Miss Petunias's hands. As if it weighed only as much as a normal muffin.

Bobert looked to Candelabra, asking for an explanation for all this, trying to ask with his eyes if she was okay. But she didn't seem to catch on, maybe because she was crying too hard.

Slowly, the realization dawned on him.

Candelabra wasn't avoiding his eyes because she was simply crying too hard. She knew exactly what was happening. Those were guilty tears she was shedding.

He knew things inside him could break. Things that weren't things at all, invisible parts of himself that could be hurt by the world. It felt like a long time ago already, but Bobert remembered how hurt he'd been by not having anyone. The way his stomach had tightened into knots when kids at school ran off to play together and left him alone during recess. He hadn't felt anything break inside him in a while, though, so this felt like something altogether new. He wanted to say it was worse, though he couldn't actually compare. What did it matter? He was broken.

Behind him came a loud rumble as the train came back

to life. He suddenly felt the weight of his feet on the ground, and the soreness in his fingers, which he didn't know what to do with, though he felt them jittering against his leg. Then the train blew its whistle and slowly pulled forward, continuing on the tracks until it revealed Shmebecca and the others. And it was clear from the look on her face that she didn't need some big speech from Mr. Eyebrows to explain what had happened.

She may not have known the details, or even realized that Candelabra was somehow involved. But she knew that they had failed. Just like Bobert knew it too.

Once the train was gone, Mr. Eyebrows had them cross the tracks to where Shmebecca and the others were. Bobert noticed that the construction crew had some sort of fancy stick with them: the Scepter of Pretty Good Control.

And now Mr. Eyebrows had both it and the Muffin of Glory.

Mr. Eyebrows was starting to talk, explaining in an overly jovial way what had happened. Which Bobert guessed made sense for where they were. But he didn't care enough to listen. He knew the important parts anyway. Candelabra had betrayed them. The plan never had a chance.

22

SHMEBECCA FELT ALL THE ENERGY LEAVE HER BODY. SHE'D always thought she'd understood what the word "crestfallen" meant. But now, as she literally fell to the ground with disappointment, she got the meaning deep in her bones.

For a moment she thought that this was where the rest of her morning would be spent: in a heap in the tall grass, her eyes shut because facing the changing world was too hard. Shmebecca thought she might never muster the energy to open them again, much less move from the spot where she'd landed. She heard the train pull away, heard the others talking, muttering, cursing. There were footsteps in the grass, people crossing the tracks to get back to the mountain.

When she finally did raise her eyelids, the first thing she saw was a bright green gentleman bug balancing itself on the tip of a blade of grass. She wanted to cup the little guy in her hand, take him home with her so she could look after him. "I'm sorry," she said out loud. "I couldn't protect you."

She didn't actually know how the bug would be affected by her failure to protect the mountain, but she knew that it was unlikely to be a good thing for the wildlife in the area. Either way, her mountain's destruction was going to happen now. She had tried to stop it, but here they were, Mr. Eyebrows and his crew, starting up their equipment to ensure no one else could try to interfere. There were two people wearing Interkingdom-Department of Magical Affairs capes holding Miss Petunias. Shmebecca didn't want to think about what they were doing there.

Maybe the mountain would burp and save itself. Maybe all the Fun Corporation employees would trip on their equipment and fall into the mud springs forever.

Looking up from the gentleman bug, Shmebecca didn't stare at the hordes of people and their machines, though. She didn't even look up at her mountain to say goodbye. She could only look at Candelabra. She would have expected herself to yell, to rage, to cry. Probably an ugly mix of all three at the same time. Instead all that came out was a quiet "Why?"

Candelabra was looking straight at Shmebecca and seemed to be blinking back a fresh round of tears. Which felt unfair. Shmebecca hadn't even had the chance to cry yet—what gave Candelabra the right to do it?

"I . . . I just had to," Candelabra said. Though the tears were starting to roll down her cheeks, she didn't wipe at them or look away from Shmebecca.

Now Shmebecca felt a hand on her shoulder, and when she turned, she saw that Bobert had come over to where she was, and that he was scowling at Candelabra. "No, you didn't!" he shouted.

Shmebecca jumped a little. She hadn't heard Bobert raise his voice like that, though she supposed she didn't know him that well. The construction crew was starting to call out instructions to each other, and their big diggers—the ones that they had been so close to rendering useless by taking away the muffin—whirred into action, tearing into the grass as they approached the trenches they'd already dug.

"Something had to change!" Candelabra shouted. "Things have been the same for so long. You have no idea how many things I tried." Her voice broke, and she had to take a breath to compose herself.

Shmebecca didn't know what Candelabra was talking about, but it seemed like a bad reason to do so much damage. "Not this!" Shmebecca yelled, no longer able to contain her own tears. "This can't ever change. It's not right." In true Jovialese fashion, her fingers now wrapped around the grass by her knees so strongly that she was sure not even a wizard with a powerful spell could have loosened her grip. Maybe that was all she had to do: hold on to the mountain for dear life. Go with it wherever they were going to move it.

"Why?" Bobert followed up, since Candelabra hadn't said anything. "Why did you do this? Why do you want things to change? Everything is fine as it is. This doesn't even affect us back home."

"She lied too!" Candelabra burst out. She wiped some snot away with her sleeve. "She said that nothing would happen to any of us, but it's not true. She's going to be fine no matter what she does. But we're Nefarians. We won't go back to our lives. Everything we have will be taken away. Why do you think these goons with the capes are here? To arrest us!"

"Hey, we're not goons," one of them muttered. "We have feelings too."

Shmebecca could feel the eyes of the Nefarians turning toward her.

"What's she talking about?" Stanbert asked.

"I know how this looks, and I'm so sorry," Candelabra continued, the gravity of her words undercut by a snot bubble growing out of her left nostril. "They said if I gave you up, they would only charge you with trespassing and conspiracy to interfere with a business that's trying to business."

Bobert exhaled beside Shmebecca, and she could hear the weight of that air leaving his lungs. "So you did give us up. You did this knowingly."

"So did she," Candelabra said again. "She was so desperate to keep her mountain from changing that she was willing to have all of us sent to a dungeon."

"I wasn't," Shmebecca said softly, which was the only way she could manage to say it. "I didn't know. I thought it would work. It could have worked if you hadn't told them."

Candelabra had no response to that. The morning air was filling with the sounds of the construction site now, and off to the side Mr. Eyebrows appeared to be giving a passionate speech, though it was unclear if anyone was listening to him. Shmebecca tried to stand up, but she still didn't have the strength. It seemed like no one in the group had the strength to move, to run, to fight. Shmayden and Shmelix were both looking at her, mouths open, and she could tell that they were hurt too.

"We don't know what will happen when we change things," Shmebecca explained. "Change brings more change, and when it comes to a volcano like Mount Saint Helenhunt, we have no idea how it will react. The situation has the chance to get very, very bad." She felt a tickle on her finger as the gentleman bug climbed onto her hand. Its antennae flicked this way and that, and Shmebecca wished she could warn it of the danger to come. She wished she knew what that danger would be. "Those were the only consequences I was thinking of."

Stanbert scoffed, but no one said anything for a while. The

morning sun got brighter, and the world was moving on with the day, even though none of the kids were ready for it.

"I'm sorry," Candelabra said finally. Now she wiped at the tears with the back of her hand, bursting her snot bubble. "But I need the lasagnanite. They don't have any back home and . . . I just need it."

"Is this about your sister?" Bobert asked. "We could have figured something out. You didn't have to do this."

"Maybe that's true," Candelabra said, sounding like the fight was leaving her. It was hard to hear her with all the hubbub happening around them. "But I was out of ideas. I went to Mr. Eyebrows first to ask for some lasagnanite. I told him why I needed it, and he said that wasn't a good enough reason." She wiped at her eyes again. "He said he needed to gain something if he was going to give something up. And I had nothing else. . . . You have to understand. Part of why I was so looking forward to this trip was that I thought I could find something here that could help Sandraliere. Help me change things for the better."

"You call this for the better?" Bobert asked, gesturing at Mr. Eyebrows, who had just wrapped up his speech to no one and was watching the machines converge on the mountain. He had his hands in his pockets and was swaying on his feet a little. Shmebecca couldn't hear him humming, but she was sure he was doing it.

THE GREATEST HEIST IN JOVIALA

As if sensing her eyes on him, he turned to look at her and the rest of the kids. Then he waved happily and called out, "If you stick around a few more minutes, you'll get to see the show!" He turned to the two caped not-goons who were holding Miss Petunias in place. "Let them stay a while. Once the show is over, you can apprehend them and do with them as you see fit."

Shmebecca looked away from the hateful man who was ruining everything she loved. Behind her were Shmelix and Shmayden, both of whom were staring daggers at Candelabra. Then there were the other Nefarians, who looked even more shocked than Shmebecca felt. Jennizabeth was crying into her hands, and Stanbert had his arms crossed in front of his chest, as if trying to protect himself from any other damage Candelabra was going to do to their operation. Or maybe he was trying to keep himself from throwing something at his friend.

Only Miss Petunias was looking on with a neutral expression, her eyes fixed on Candelabra. The first of the explosions boomed nearby, the sound muffled by the dirt. It shook the ground, and an earthquake followed shortly after, the two as clearly distinguishable as witnessing a stampede of rat-birds versus being caught in the middle of one.

"I don't really know if it's better," Candelabra said, her eyes downcast. "I hope it is. I really do. Not just for me and my sister. But for everyone here, too." She looked up directly at Shmebecca then, as if the words were meant for her alone.

And Shmebecca had to admit that for a second she felt for Candelabra. Or, at least, she could recognize that whatever Candelabra had felt that had driven her to do this was real, and deep-seated. It didn't help Shmebecca at all, but there it was anyway.

"You know what this feels like, don't you?" Bobert said. His hand was still on Shmebecca's shoulder, which was more helpful than she would have thought it would be. It made her feel like she could at least survive this. What came next, she wasn't sure. But for now it helped to have his gentle support there, if only as a reminder that she wasn't alone.

"Don't say it," Candelabra said, more tears coming to her eyes.

"I don't want to, Candy. But if it looks like an evil scheme and smells like an evil scheme . . . how does the rest of the saying go?" Bobert turned to look at the other Nefarians. "Something about it being a duck?"

The others just shook their heads, and every one of them looked the way Shmebecca felt. Torn up and scared and angry. Candelabra lowered her head as a sob tore through her.

"I'm sorry about your sister," Bobert said. "But you could have come to us." He gestured at himself, and at Stanbert and

Jennizabeth behind him. "We could have found lasagnanite some other way. Instead you chose to scheme—"

"Don't say that," Candelabra interrupted, though her voice was drowned out by another explosion, this one making Shmebecca jump. There was a terrifying, impossibly loud groan afterward, and it seemed to be coming from the mountain itself.

"Perfectly normal!" Mr. Eyebrows shouted at them. "Totally Fine! We were expecting this. This next bit is going to be really exciting. And loud! I hope that your little plan included some earplugs." He grinned as he pulled out a pair from his pants pockets. The interkingdom officers shared a look, and Mr. Eyebrows cackled. "That's okay—I've got some for you! This is all the most normal thing that could be happening, I assure you."

Now the explosions ramped up, with one every fifteen seconds or so. Shmebecca couldn't bear to look, but she couldn't pry her eyes away, either. At the base of the mountain, the bursts of flame and smoke were coming in a straight line, shooting out dirt and debris.

They just kept coming and coming, all around the mountain. Then, just when she thought the terrible commotion would stop, another round came—this time from deeper within the mountain, she could tell. They were cutting it all the way across, as she'd imagined. Then they would lift it up and away, though where to, Shmebecca still didn't know. Not that it mattered much.

Suddenly Shmebecca could no longer bear to look. After easing the bug onto the ground, she let go of the grass and lifted herself up. The ground kept shaking, and the air was warm with the heat of explosions and the magic used to lift the mountain. Still, a shiver ran through Shmebecca, followed by a wave of exhaustion. She just wanted to be home, in bed, under her covers.

Her friends seemed frozen in place, watching the explosions they'd worked so hard to prevent coming in a barrage. Most of them had their hands over their ears. They looked as tired as she felt, and she knew they'd stick around as long as she did. "I'd like to go home," she announced, looking at the interkingdom officers. "You all should too. Who knows what we'll have to deal with the next few hours."

The officers didn't hear her at first, because of the earplugs they'd used and the explosions they'd used them for. She had to repeat herself, and something about how she delivered the statement seemed to scare the officers. The redheaded one—KittyKat, according to his name tag—gave a nod. "The Jovialese children are free to go. The Nefarians will have to come with us and await criminal extradition back to Nefaria."

THE GREATEST HEIST IN JOVIALA

"Oh my god, they're going to juice us!" Stanbert cried out, horror in his voice.

"What? No," Bobert said. "'Extradition' means they're going to send us back home."

"Oh. Okay. I guess that's better."

Another explosion rang out, and Officer KittyKat left Miss Petunias and walked toward the children. "All right, let's go," he said in a Southern Jovialese drawl. "Everyone stay in my sight. Head to town—I'll be following."

As if broken free from a spell, the other kids turned away from the mountain. They started gathering their bags and ropes and their various disguises, most of which they hadn't had to use. Shmebecca almost wanted to laugh at how many supplies she'd brought, how hopeful she'd been a few hours ago that she could interfere with something so much larger than herself. She should have known that if Joviala had allowed something like this to change, she wasn't going to be able to do anything about it.

Bobert and Candelabra were the only ones who hadn't moved at all. They were staring at each other, a silent conversation passing between them. Miss Petunias was standing in between them, as if trying to ease the tension. The interkingdom officer holding on to her looked around awkwardly, shuffling his feet. Shmebecca approached them, looking at Bobert but unable to bring herself to look at Candelabra directly. "You coming?"

"Yeah," Bobert said quickly, turning away from Candelabra swiftly, in a way that almost made Shmebecca feel bad for her. Almost.

"Shmebecca, I'm sorry," Candelabra said, tears still in her voice. Probably on her face, too, but Shmebecca wasn't about to confirm that. She was keeping her eyes on the horizon, where the hints of sunrise were starting to bloom in the clouds. Pinks and oranges, like little explosions in the sky. A rat-bird called out its usual morning song, or at least the first verse. They were famously long songs that usually had at least twelve verses.

Bobert ran back to get his own things, mostly his backpack, which was still soaked from emptying out the piranha tank. A few moments later he was at her side, giving her another squeeze on the shoulder before letting her guide them to town quietly.

For a long part of the walk, the explosions rang out nearly as loud as if they were still right beside the mountain. A few more earthquakes hit too, during which Shmebecca only slowed down in order to find her footing.

Once it was quiet, Shmebecca could hear the others' footsteps dragging along behind. She could hear Miss Petunias and the interkingdom officers chatting amicably, though her mind was churning too much to pay attention.

THE GREATEST HEIST IN JOVIALA

In town there weren't a lot of people out and about yet; the sun hadn't fully come up after all. But those who were already awake looked every now and then in the direction of Mount Saint Helenhunt, their brows furrowed. Shmebecca resisted the urge to follow their gazes, worried that if she did, her mountain might not be there anymore.

23

Candelabra tried not to think about what Bobert had said, or the look on Shmebecca's face before they'd all walked away, the hulking and caped interkingdom officers following, hands over their holstered wands.

Instead she stood next to Mr. Eyebrows and kept her eyes on the activity on the mountain, waiting for them to do whatever they had to do so she could get the lasagnanite and go home.

The explosions had stopped a while ago, and now the enchanted lifting machines were moving in. There were about twenty of them positioned along the base of the mountain. They looked like the drawings in the schematics Shmebecca had shown them: big mechanical hands-on wheels, powerful enough to move the earth itself. Which was exactly what they were going to do.

Most of the wildlife in the area had fled hours ago, when the final stage of Mr. Eyebrows's plan began, thanks to Candelabra's

THE GREATEST HEIST IN JOVIALA

interference in the heist. There'd been explosions in preparation the whole time they were on the train. Still, every now and then a rat-bird flew off into the sky, cawing its beautiful soprano song sadly into the morning air, or occasionally getting into a rap battle with a flying goat, though Candelabra wasn't in the mood to listen.

The deal she'd struck with Mr. Eyebrows meant that as soon as the mountain was moved, a group would search for the first batch of lasagnanite and give her enough to break the spell on Sandraliere's painting. Then she would get on a boat that would take her back to Nefaria. At first she had hoped to keep her involvement with Mr. Eyebrows secret. She was going to betray her friends (but in doing so, secure lighter punishments for them), then claim some sort of emergency so her Nefarian chaperones would send her back home. That plan was clearly ruined now, but she had managed to convince Mr. Eyebrows to get her a ticket for safe passage home. Alone.

Tears stung her eyes and she wiped them away as a chorus of shouts filled the air. It seemed the machine operators were going down the line announcing that they were in position. Mr. Eyebrows hummed happily beside her, and even though Candelabra wanted what was about to happen, she wasn't thrilled to hear him gloating. She moved her arms out as if she was yawning and elbowed him in the side.

"Sorry," she grumbled.

"Quite all right! We're all very excited. This part should be fun to watch." He called over two hard-hatted men, and one woman wearing a softer-looking hat. She was also wearing the leather gloves the caped men had brought, which allowed her to easily carry the case with the muffin. Candelabra recalled the look on her friends' faces and was tempted to reach for it and run into the woods. But that clearly was not a good plan.

The adults chatted quietly for a moment; then the woman holding the muffin set it down on the ground. She pulled off the gloves and handed them to Mr. Eyebrows, who couldn't resist dancing as he slipped them on. Then he reached down and picked up the Muffin of Glory, giving the glass case a little wipe with the hem of his shirt, even though it was already very shiny.

He gave her a wink after polishing the glass, and then they both braced as another earthquake shook everything around. This time Candelabra could saw a crack forming about a hundred yards away. She found herself wanting the ground to open up and swallow all the machines, though immediately she scolded herself. How would that help her and Sandraliere? She still didn't have the lasagnanite in hand.

When the shaking ended, Mr. Eyebrows brushed himself off, winked again, and then walked toward the scepter, the top of which was goblet-shaped, where the muffin fit in. The scepter had a sort of tube that connected to all the lifting machines, which was how, Mr. Eyebrows explained gleefully, they could draw the necessary power to lift the mountain.

All the other workers stopped what they were doing to watch him approach with the muffin held high above his head. They were all smiling, and some applauded gently. Candelabra rolled her eyes. "Just get on with it!" she shouted, drawing some frowns from the two construction workers closest by.

Mr. Eyebrows didn't seem to hear her or didn't much care. He showed off the muffin to the left, then to the right, then pumped it in the air a few times. Candelabra took a step forward, half meaning to run toward him and place the muffin in the scepter herself, get it over with. She didn't care that she didn't have the gloves. She'd rip them off his stupid, overly gesticulating hands. Her friends were being marched toward a prison because of her—she couldn't handle watching someone be happy right now.

Then Mr. Eyebrows took a couple of bows and plopped the muffin right in. It actually made a plop as it fell into place, a comical sound that didn't quite fit with so momentous an act. Candelabra braced herself for what would happen next. At first there was nothing but a slight whir. "Is that it?" the woman with the tarantula-shaped hair asked loudly. Candelabra could see a few of the construction workers shrugging.

Then there was a flash of light that caused Mr. Eyebrows to shield his eyes. A golden beam shot upward from the scepter, then filled the tube that connected to the lifting machines. One by one they started glowing as well, then whirring, until the area around Candelabra was as bright and loud as if Mount Saint Helenhunt were erupting. Now beams of light shot forward from the machines directly into the holes that had been blown into the side of the mountain. They didn't make any noise, surprisingly, though Candelabra could feel a heat emanating from the light beams, warming up the pleasant early-morning air.

The golden light burrowed its way into the mountain, and for a brief moment it seemed like the beams were just going to get swallowed up and nothing would happen. Part of Candelabra almost hoped that was how things would turn out.

There was a terrific ripping sound, and the hardest earthquake Candelabra had felt yet dropped her to her knees. She was thankful that she wasn't in town, because being in a building would have been terrifying, no matter how well-prepared Jovialese buildings supposedly were. She hoped Bobert and the others hadn't made it to town yet.

The crack that had formed in the ground had spread further, and for a moment Candelabra thought that was the noise she'd heard. But then the tearing grew louder and louder, so loud that she felt like she was inside the noise itself, like she would never hear anything else again. It was so loud that it caused a wind to blow across the valley. Even the smallest insects were bolting now, a tiny stampede frantically fleeing their home.

Like everyone else, Candelabra covered her ears with her hands, trying to shut out as much of the terrible sound as possible. It felt like the world itself was coming apart.

Then the noise stopped, and Mount Saint Helenhunt came loose.

It hovered about ten feet off the ground, enough for Candelabra to be able to see what was on the other side of the mountain: some more construction equipment and a smattering of Mr. Eyebrows's people, who were no longer smiling and were slowly backing away. Some were already running.

Dirt and rocks cascaded from the mountain to the ground where it had been, along with something liquid and glowing that Candelabra hadn't ever seen before. "What is that?" she asked the woman with the dancing-tarantula-shaped hair.

"Oh, just some mountain juice!" the woman responded cheerily, shouting because even though the tearing had stopped, there was still a lot of noise coming from the whirring scepter, the machines, and the rocks falling to the ground. "Nothing to worry about!"

"I hate how often you people say that," Candelabra grumbled. "Will someone go get my lasagnanite so I can get out of here?"

"That's them now!" The woman pointed at a group of people

wearing yellow hard hats and puffy suits, who were waddling in the direction of the torn earth where the mountain had been just a few minutes ago. Meanwhile, the lifting machines were rolling toward the east, their beams still pointed at the mountain, carrying it away to the planned resting site, wherever that was. Candelabra could hardly believe she was seeing a mountain being moved, but she supposed she'd seen lots of incredible things in her life.

It took almost an hour for the lasagnanite crew to do whatever they needed to do, squatting where the grassy field met the earthy rubble where the mountain used to be. An hour of sitting with herself and her thoughts, with the memory of the betrayal, the hurt, on her friends' faces. She wished her mind were a faucet she could just shut off, at least until she was back home with Sandraliere.

There were tufts of steam and smoke coming from the ground, and every fifteen minutes or so another earthquake made the crew stop fiddling with their tools. They didn't seem overly worried, so Candelabra tried to take that as a sign that she shouldn't be either.

Finally, after Candelabra had attempted a nap in the grass, and then accepted a breakfast sandwich from a friendly construction worker, she saw one of the crew members approach Mr. Eyebrows with a glass beaker, in which Candelabra could see two shiny, fist-sized black rocks.

THE GREATEST HEIST IN JOVIALA

She ran over to meet him, her hands out, expecting him to put up a fight of some sort, or renege on their deal. It would be typical of a man in power to try to trick her somehow, to find some loophole that meant he wouldn't actually give her the lasagnanite. She would get to hold it for only three minutes. Or he wouldn't give her enough to break Sandraliere's spell. Somehow, everything she had done would have been for nothing. She would have betrayed Bobert and Shmebecca and a whole kingdom for nothing.

But Mr. Eyebrows handed it over quickly. "Enjoy your casserole!" he said with his unnatural all-teeth smile.

"Oh," Candelabra said, knowing that the surprise she was feeling came from having grown up in Nefaria, where she absolutely would have been tricked in some way or another.

She waited for a second, as if giving him space to change his mind. Then some part of her whispered that there was no trickery coming because she was the one who had committed the evil act. This man wasn't even capable of scheming in a nefarious way. He was doing harm, but he didn't even know that was what he was doing. She was the one who had purposely done something she'd known would hurt others. Would hurt her friends.

She quickly shut up that part of her brain (or at least tried to) by sticking the rocks in her bag, turning around, and breaking into a run toward the tree line.

She didn't know what exactly she was going to do to get home, but she knew she couldn't be here anymore. She'd found a way to change Sandraliere's situation, and if that came with unintended consequences, well, then, she would just go be with her sister. She would free her from her canvas prison and the two of them could go anywhere they wanted.

24

THE PEOPLE OF JOVIALA WERE ABOUT TO PUT THEIR strong fingers to good use. They were going to hang on to door frames to avoid getting tossed to the ground. They were going to grip the little gaps in tree bark, hiding behind the trunks to avoid getting struck by flying debris. They were going to hold on for dear life to the grass so that they would not fall into the cracks opening in the earth all around them.

They had survived many natural disasters, of course. They had practice doing all these things. But something about that late morning felt different. It felt like all those disasters they'd lived through before were striking at once. And to add to the sense of foreboding, the mountain whose shadow they were used to living in was gone.

Not that they could necessarily tell. It had been clear for a couple of hours earlier in the morning that something was off with Mount Saint Helenhunt, and some of them had taken note. But they'd been going about their usual day and hadn't thought much about the plume of smoke that had started to form where the mountain used to be. Back then—it already felt like a clear *before*, as opposed to the obvious *after* they were living in now—they couldn't have known what was coming.

They didn't know they'd be hanging on to their loved ones, to the possessions they cared most about.

At Shmebecca's school, the students were unaware of what their classmate and the visitors had been up to. And they were blissfully unaware of what was coming. They'd been using their strong fingers the way they normally did: for booger-flicking competitions in the field, using the rock-climbing wall, swinging expertly on the monkey bars.

After the failed heist, it wasn't like Bobert and the others could just hide under the covers and wallow. The interkingdom officers led the kids to the school first so they could inform Mr. Gigglebutt and Principal Shmishmash about what had happened and that the student exchange was going to get cut short.

Bobert and the others were lying in the grass near the picnic tables, one of the officers sitting nearby watching over them. They all needed to sleep, but none had managed to. Understandably. Anyone in Joviala who had hoped to sleep in that morning was in for the very roughest of awakenings.

Bobert still couldn't believe what Candelabra had done. He was lying there watching ashes rise up in the sky and then saunter down like malicious snowflakes. One landed on his cheek, and he wiped it away, forgetting that all that would do was leave a gray streak on his face.

It was the last semi-peaceful moment he would have for a while, and he didn't even know it. None of them did. Not even Shmebecca, who had already suspected things were going to get bad, had any idea how bad they would get, and how quickly.

At that moment, where Mount Saint Helenhunt used to be, the earth was sending up angry eruptions of molten rock and poisonous gas. Materials that had been safely and happily contained within and beneath the mountain now had nowhere to circulate.

From a distance, Mr. Eyebrows furrowed his brow. He turned to his assistant, Shmindy. "Is this still all Totally Fine and Well?"

She flipped through the papers attached to her clipboard. "Um—um—" she stammered. "It doesn't say it here. . . ."

A rock the size of her head went zinging past them, close enough that they could smell the hair on their arms burning. Mr. Eyebrows cleared his throat. "Right, well, maybe it's time for a lunch break."

Another rock shot up from the ground, this one with a tail of fire as it rose, disappeared into the ash cloud, and then came zooming back toward the construction site. It whistled on its descent, and all the workers ran for safety. It came crashing down mere feet away from one of the diggers.

"Ring the bell!" Mr. Eyebrows exclaimed, already speed-walking in the other direction, toward where they'd parked the train. "Quickly! Quickly! Everything is Totally Fine and Well, but we should all go to lunch far, far away from here! Right this second, please!"

When kids at school started screaming and running for cover, that was when Shmebecca and the others finally sat up. "I knew it," Shmebecca said. "I knew this was going to happen. They didn't listen."

Bobert knew that there was nothing he could say that would make her feel better about that. She was going to be angry for a while, and she probably deserved to be angry. He hoped it wasn't something she would carry with her forever.

The truth was that he was angry at her, too. Her offense might not have been as egregious as Candelabra's, but not telling them about the consequences was still a bad thing to do. He wished she'd just been honest with them instead of changing the subject every time it came up.

For now he climbed to his feet and then reached his hand down to help her up. He didn't want to talk to her, but he wasn't about to let her just stay there in the middle of what sounded like the apocalypse.

As she took his hand, Bobert noticed that there were little fires raining down nearby. He looked toward the mountain—or where it used to be, anyway—and saw that the plume of smoke was much, much bigger now. There were also bright orange streaks cutting through the clouds. He wasn't sure which of the two sights was scarier, but he didn't want to stick around and find out.

"Can we get to safety?" Bobert asked the officer.

He'd been reading a book and just now seemed to notice the chaos happening around them. "Yeah, that'd probably be best," he said.

"Don't have to tell me twice," Stanbert said. "Are there any rat-birds around that might want to carry us all the way to Nefaria?"

"They're smarter than we are," Shmebecca said, brushing herself off. "They left a long time ago."

Inside, the teachers were corralling kids toward the disaster safety zone. It was an impressive space, so reinforced that Bobert couldn't even feel the ground shaking, which it hadn't stopped doing since they'd left the mountain. There was a full auditorium in there, where someone who could only be the drama teacher was putting on a puppet show to comfort the younger kids, even though no one seemed to be paying attention.

Immediately upon entering, Bobert and the others were handed blankets, water, and snacks. They were told not to worry, even though the crying from others was echoing off the walls, and Principal Shmishmash did not sound very convincing. Apparently, she was too concerned with everything going on to admonish the kids for what they'd done the night before. Bobert wasn't about to complain.

There was a cafeteria, a game room, and even a pool with multiple waterslides. This was definitely better than whatever dungeon was awaiting them when they got home. But almost none of the amenities were being taken advantage of, not even by the Jovialese kids, who were used to disasters.

It was like they knew what was going to come. Like they knew the earth would take revenge on Mr. Eyebrows and the Fun Corporation, on all the people who'd ignored Shmebecca's pleas. The mountain (or the place where the mountain used to be) had no feelings one way or another. It was not angry. It simply reacted to change. The people around it had changed its circumstances, and so it was going to react.

Now the people of Joviala were going to have to react as well. They were going to have to take shelter from the volcanic bombs that were raining down for miles. They were going to have to find cleaner air to breathe to avoid the poisonous

THE GREATEST HEIST IN JOVIALA

fumes in the ash cloud, which was not just climbing high up into the sky but spreading outward in all directions, wreaking havoc on most living things that couldn't run away. It was also dirtying practically every wall and window it came in contact with, but almost everyone agreed that was low on the priorities list.

The people of Joviala were lucky to have places to shelter them. They sometimes took them for granted during the small disasters that could happen on any given day throughout the year. It was just like having a bed or food at home. Anyone could forget to be happy for everyday comforts, even if they were necessities.

But on that day, they were thankful for the land they lived in. They were thankful for their strong fingers, which held them in place. They were thankful that, even if where they lived wasn't perfect, it didn't have the flaws some other places had. And they had these places to protect themselves when the land lashed out at them.

Mr. Eyebrows was in his bunker at home, finally feeling safe. He was looking at the contracts he'd signed with the construction workers, making sure he wasn't responsible in case of disaster. He was reading the fine print to see how long he would have to wait to hire new ones.

Shmarcos and Shmary, who were watching over the twins that day, since Shmorris and Shborris had caught a cold, carried the boys down to the basement—calmly, so as not to scare them. They thought about Shmebecca, hoping she was safe and sound where she was. They each remembered the things Shmebecca had said at the town hall that day. Her mountain, she'd called it. How it had saved her life, and how she needed to save it back.

They wondered if she'd been right. Wondered *how* right she'd been in that unfortunate, bumbling speech of hers. How bad was this going to get? And why had they been so sure that everything would be fine, when their daughter had tried to warn them otherwise?

25

CANDELABRA CAUGHT THE EARLIEST BOAT HEADED toward Nefaria. She'd gathered her things from Shmebecca's house, left a note so no one would worry, and walked down to the docks.

Even though there were signs of the coming disaster, no one was trying to flee Joviala. Not yet, anyway. In the hours and days to come, the docks would start to fill up with families holding as much as they could carry. They'd be going to stay with cousins who lived farther north, or friends who lived in another kingdom. They would choose to be strangers in strange lands, as long as they were safer than at home. Anyone who still had a functioning boat would be called on to help get people to safety.

For now, though, Candelabra found a spot on a boat easily, and the ride was just a little bumpy. There was a smell of sulfur in the air, and water sometimes sloshed over the side of the boat, so Candelabra had to lift her feet so her shoes wouldn't get soaked. Two passengers nearby—traders on the way to Los Angsteles, from what she'd overheard—complained about motion sickness.

But the rocky ride was helpful for her. It gave her something to focus on. She could pretend that the feeling in her stomach was due entirely to motion sickness. She clutched the beaker with the lasagnanite, repeating to herself that this had been worth it.

When the boat finally docked in Nefaria, Candelabra was exhausted. She hadn't slept at all on the journey, and that was adding to the surreal experience of being back home. She'd expected it to be changed, somehow. But it was exactly the same as when she'd left almost a week ago, down to the shady people hanging around the dock offering good rates to convert her Jovialese money into Nefarian dollars. There was something almost comforting about being greeted by a scheme right away.

When one of the dock schemers approached her, she didn't even hiss at him, as was common when you knew someone was trying to pull one over on you in Nefaria. She just laughed and shook her head, and as she walked away she felt like weeping, not for the first time that day. There were news criers on the dock too, and though she heard them saying things about disaster in Joviala, she hurried past them.

When she saw her house again, she nearly crumpled in a

THE GREATEST HEIST IN JOVIALA

heap. She had to stand there for a moment and just look at it, almost in disbelief. When she walked in, everything would finally change—in the way she wanted it to. The thought briefly smothered her guilt with its joy.

She ended up running the rest of the way, eager to be inside, eager to shut the rest of the world out. This was what mattered, just her and Sandraliere.

She pushed the door open and tossed her bag on the floor, bringing into the living room the groceries she'd picked up along the way. There it was. The painting her sister had been trapped in for over two years now. "Guess who!" she called out.

Her sister didn't appear for a minute, which meant she was probably out gathering apples or fishing in the creek. Little did she know it would be the last time she had to do those things in her painted world. Candelabra smiled at the realization, picturing her sister's face when she found out she could leave. She made a little more noise, in case Sandraliere was asleep in her cottage, then left three pillows stacked on the couch in front of the fireplace, her usual sign to her sister that she was home.

In the kitchen she set two pots of water to boil. One was for the cat-hair pasta she was going to make for dinner, since it was Sandraliere's favorite. The other was for the lasagnanite.

She went back to the living room and made a fire, then reread the instructions for using the lasagnanite to break spells.

By the time Sandraliere appeared, groggily exiting her

cottage and rubbing her eyes, Candelabra had already finished preparing the pasty lasagnanite elixir and was spreading it around the edges of the picture frame. "What are you doing?" Sandraliere said. "Aren't you supposed to be in Happyland for another two days?"

"Don't worry about that," Candelabra said, rubbing more of the paste on the frame.

Sandraliere wrinkled her nose. "What's that smell?"

"I'm making cat-hair pasta!"

"Okay, jerk, thanks a lot for rubbing that in while I eat my six trillionth apple. But no, that's not what I'm talking about." She sniffed again, looking comically like a rabbit with her nose scrunched up. Candelabra could hardly contain her excitement at the thought that she would get to see that nose in person soon, not through the filter of a painting. "It's something . . . earthier. Not really in a bad way, but not in a good way, either."

"I think what you're smelling is a surprise."

"Is that some way of saying you farted? You know I don't learn new slang in here." She sighed and plopped down on the grass, playing with the tall oat blades that she always ran her fingers through mindlessly when talking with Candelabra.

Candelabra just giggled and set down the brush she'd been using for the paste. She took two steps back and pulled out the piece of paper with the curse-breaking spell. She cleared her throat, prompting a raised eyebrow from her sister.

"Okay, you're weirding me out a little. You're not gonna start singing, are you? Our family was not meant for singing. Or are you going to recite a poem? Ooh! It's a poem about how much you love me and how I'm the best older sister of all time, right?" Sandraliere sat up straight and clapped her hands, like a kid waiting for a read-along at a library to begin.

"Shush," Candelabra said. "I'm going to say some weird things, and then . . ." The grin that spread across her face was so big it interrupted her. "Well, then you'll see," she said.

It struck her that this was the second time in as many years that she was involved in the breaking of a curse. Then that made her think of Bobert and the others, still back in Joviala. But she didn't want to think about them right now. So she started reading. She didn't look up from the paper once, afraid that she'd say the words wrong and that it would ruin the process. Or that she would see it not working at all.

She powered through the four stanzas of mostly gibberish and finished by taking in a deep breath. She closed her eyes and held it, waiting to feel something shifting in the air, waiting for a magical *pop!* or *zing!* or even a *kablooey!*

Sensing none of that, Candelabra slowly opened one eye. Through her lashes she first saw the painting. It was still there, its frame covered in the black paste, which was starting to drip off the sides. Other than that, it looked the same. Same little cottage, same yellow-tinged meadow with the creek in the background, same blue sky.

Except her sister wasn't there anymore.

Candelabra opened her eyes all the way and stepped up to the painting, scanning for a sign of her sister. Maybe she was just messing with her, hiding in the tall grass? Or she'd run out of frame or something?

"No, no, no," Candelabra said, looking back down at the instructions for the spell. Where had she gone wrong? Was there some part of the lasagnanite that refused to break a curse if the person using it was unworthy? Was it not going to give Candelabra her sister back because of what she'd done to her temporary sister in Joviala? Had she sold out her friends for nothing?

"Peekaboo," a voice said right in her ear.

Candelabra jumped, even though the joy was already coursing through her veins, quieting her earlier thoughts. She had not heard her sister's voice that close in over two years. She turned around, not fully believing that it had worked until Sandraliere was wrapping her in her arms.

It had worked. It had really worked. She had made it happen.

They were both crying, alternating between big, heaving sobs and bursts of laughter. "How did you just do that?"

Sandraliere asked, holding her tight enough that the air got pushed out of Candelabra's lungs.

"Ew, your snot is getting on my neck," she said when she'd recovered.

"I've been dying to get my snot on your neck for two years. And you know you've been dying to feel it too."

Candelabra laughed and said "ew" again, but she made no move to wipe at her neck or move her sister away. It felt so good to actually hold her sister, smell her, accidentally get her hair in her mouth as she laughed with relief. "I can't believe we're actually hugging."

"Of course we're hugging, you goof. Did you really forget I'm an obsessive hugger? And nuzzler, tickler, hand-holder?" Sandraliere said, performing each action as she said it. "And I haven't had the pleasure of doing any of it for two years." Her voice broke on the last sentence, and the sisters squeezed each other tighter, as if scared that they might lose each other again.

After a few moments, Sandraliere pulled away ever so slightly to cup Candelabra's cheek in her hand. "But seriously, how did you do that? How am I free? Why are you back?"

The answer was too long and complicated and hard to get into without crying for another thirty seconds. "I'll tell you over some cat-hair pasta," she said. As if on cue, she could hear the sauce simmering in the kitchen.

"Okay," Sandraliere said. "Meanwhile, I am going to use a real bathroom. I can't tell you how excited I am to do that."

"Great, I don't want to hear about it," Candelabra said, still holding on tightly to her sister, not knowing if she would ever let go.

Eventually she did, though, and when they'd finished eating and Sandraliere had asked for the six hundredth time or so how it was that she'd broken the curse, Candelabra found herself on the verge of tears again, and not the happy ones this time.

But there was no point hiding them, no point keeping anything to herself. She had her sister again, and this was the exact kind of conversation that she'd wanted to have her favorite person in front of her for. She was the only person who could possibly make her feel better.

She told her everything she'd lived through over the past week. Her hope that the trip to Joviala would provide some miracle cure. Hearing Shmebecca explain what she'd learned about her mountain, feeling sure that she was in the middle of another evil scheme that she wanted to fix, even if she had originally wanted to just enjoy the newness that Joviala had to offer. Then she'd learned about lasagnanite, and that had given her hope to have her real sister back, even if it was going to break her host sister's heart. She told Sandraliere about going to Mr. Eyebrows for a deal.

By the time she was done reliving it, she felt like she really had just gone through it all again. The adrenaline that had kicked in upon arriving home had run out, and now all she wanted to do was to get in bed and sleep the next few days away. Preferably with her sister not leaving her side the whole time.

Sandraliere had sat across from her quietly, listening, taking small sips of water, occasionally asking a clarifying question. Now she stood up and moved to the chair beside Candelabra, whose heart soared. Her sister! Next to her again!

"First of all, *daughter*," she said, smirking. Candelabra laughed through her tears and told her to shut up. "Thank you. Truly, thank you for caring enough to want me here with you. I don't know how you turned into the incredible, brave person you are. I'm in awe of you and the things you've already done in your young life."

Candelabra had to choke down another sobbing chuckle at that.

"I love you," Sandraliere went on, turning Candelabra's chair so that they were face-to-face, and putting both hands on Candelabra's shoulders. "And while I'm very glad to be here, with you, touching you, eating cat-hair pasta with you—"

"How'd it turn out, by the way?" Candelabra said, wiping at her nose, not caring that she got snot on her sleeve. She was one big ball of snot at this point.

"Hon, it was the first thing I've eaten in the real world in two years. It was the best meal I've ever had. But no more interruptions." She pointed a stern finger in her sister's face, then sighed, running a hand through her hair. Candelabra found herself tensing up, recognizing that Sandraliere's tone was shifting. That was one thing that had not been lost throughout her time in the painting (a time which was now over!): her sister's shift in tone.

Finally, it seemed like Sandraliere found the words that she was looking for. "My dear sister, even though I'm happy to be here, you messed up."

She let the weight of those words land. Which they did, right in Candelabra's chest with enough force to make her feel like she'd lost her breath. She looked into her lap, a place she'd been staring at an awful lot the last couple of days, since she had known what she was going to do.

"You probably know you messed up, don't you?" Sandraliere said. She scooted closer and grabbed Candelabra's chin gingerly with her thumb and forefinger, tilting her head up so that they were eye to eye. Somewhere nearby, a singing mountain spider was performing its nightly soprano song. Candelabra hadn't ever thought of it as a mournful song, just a pretty one. But now it seemed like the perfect encapsulation of what she was feeling.

"I was just so sick of not having you." Her voice sounded so small, alien to her. "I didn't mean to harm anyone."

"But you did," Sandraliere said, matter-of-fact. "And I may not be the most involved parent—"

Candelabra rolled her eyes. "You're my sister, for the last time."

"Yes, thank you, I prefer that too. But, as weird as it is for me to admit it, I am *also* your parent. And even though for the past two years I raised you from over there"—she nodded her head in the direction of the living room—"I raised you to be better than to just walk away from harm you caused. So did our parents."

Candelabra looked away, reaching for the crumpled napkin next to her empty dinner bowl. She'd devoured the cat-hair pasta, hungry from the long day of travel and everything that had come before. Now she couldn't imagine eating ever again. "What can I do, though?"

"Come," Sandraliere said, patting her knee, and then she stood up and headed toward the living room. "I've been dreaming about having a couch again for so long." She grabbed two logs from the pile next to the fire and tossed them in, then plopped herself down on the couch, sighing with pleasure. She gestured to the empty seat next to her.

Candelabra bit her lip, staring at the flames rising from the embers, licking at the new logs. In her mind's eye she could see the same thing happening all over Joviala. But what good did picturing that do for her?

She joined Sandraliere, nuzzling into her, chewing on her own thumb. Usually, her brain was quick to think of solutions. And if not solutions, then at least actions. Some series of steps she could take that would make her feel like she was going to fix whatever the problem was. But now all she could do was picture Joviala, and the looks on Bobert's and Shmebecca's faces.

She craned her neck up to look at her sister, who despite looking extremely content, gave Candelabra a little smack on the back of the head, then pulled her in closer.

"What can I do?" Candelabra asked again.

"I don't know, love," Sandraliere said. "But you have your big sister here to help now. We'll figure something out."

26

IN A DINGY CASTLE DUNGEON ON THE OUTSKIRTS OF THE town of Nefaria, there was a room that had been cleared out of its previous torture devices and now had six chairs in a circle, plus a table with an assortment of cold and disappointing snacks.

In one of those six chairs sat a woman from the Interkingdom Department of Magical Affairs, and she was currently nodding pleasantly while making pointed eye contact with the man who was speaking. He had been speaking for a long time. A considerable portion of that time had just been him listing all his nicknames.

But, to his credit, he was now talking about what he was supposed to: his journey toward rehabilitation. Almost everyone in the room was required to be there. The only one who was there by choice was a Jovialese woman who just liked getting to know people and came to listen to others' stories.

"And are you still having evil thoughts?" the interkingdom

agent facilitating the meeting asked, interrupting the wizard with the matted gray beard and the hand gestures that threatened to severely injure all those around him.

"Excuse me!" the wizard shouted, putting a hand on his chest like he couldn't believe what he was hearing. "I never once had evil thoughts!" He reached to his side where wizards usually kept their wands, then started patting himself all over.

"Matt, we talked about this. Take a breath."

The animated wizard stammered a response asking how dare they take his wand away, then caught himself and breathed in slowly through his mouth. "Exploding never helped anybody," he repeated a few times, clearly a mantra. Everyone in the room had a mantra. Once he had calmed himself, he looked around the room and apologized. "I just don't like to call them evil thoughts. I had some misguided plans in my life, but the intention was never fully evil. Just mostly selfish."

"What about your plan to shave all the kittens in Nefaria?" Delillian the Dragon Slayer asked.

"That would have been hilarious and you know it!" Matt snapped. He immediately raised his hands in another apology and continued more calmly. "All I'm trying to say is I've made progress. And I have been better at recognizing plans that could possibly harm others, even if they would be totally awesome in other ways."

"Have you been making amends?" the snail-person to his

THE GREATEST HEIST IN JOVIALA

left asked. The snail-person was mild mannered, but everyone in the room knew that meant that he'd probably been the most evil among them before being rehabilitated.

"Yes, yes," Matt grumbled, giving the impression that it had been a chore, even though he'd actually been enjoying rectifying things among his past "victims." He didn't like to think of them as such, but in his journey away from evil schemes, he'd come to realize that he had left a wake of damaged people behind him. Not as many as he thought, and not even as damaged as the authorities claimed, but still, there were quite a few of them. "There are just a handful left to go." He sighed deeply, thinking of how long it had taken him so far.

"The gumball kids?" Delillian asked.

"The gumball kids." Matt nodded. "The royal courts have forbidden me from contacting most of them, so I've had to go through a lot of hoops."

"Ah, yes, the Hoops of Judgment," the snail-person said. "Can you believe they made me jump through them too? Not exactly understanding of my physical constraints. . . ."

"How many left to go?" the interkingdom agent asked Matt.

Matt reached into his robes for the list he carried with him wherever he went (not that he got to go many places these days). It was the only thing he could consistently find in his robes. It was a pocket scroll, and over the past year he'd managed to tear it a few times, spill more than one beverage on it, and even catch it a little bit on fire. At the very bottom were just a few names left uncrossed. *Bobert Bougainvillea, Candelabra Dangling, Imogene Petunias.* "Not too many," Matt said. "Though I don't know if I'll ever see them again."

At that moment, the door pushed open.

27

After three days of waiting out the destruction in the safety of the Jovialese school, the students were finally going to be allowed to emerge back to the surface. The word spread quickly throughout the school's bunker and eventually reached Shmebecca, who for three days had been curled up on the floor, barely eating, only occasionally getting up to use the bathroom. The Nefarians, Shmelix, and Shmayden had stayed nearby, keeping watch over her, trying to assure her that everything was going to be okay—even as the interkingdom officers hovered, ensuring that they weren't going to try to use the natural disaster(s) to escape.

But the whispered rumors that the doors were opening did nothing to perk her up. "What's the point?" she mumbled, not bothering to uncurl herself from the pile of blankets she'd burrowed into. The blankets felt safe and warm, and they were the only place where, for the last three days, her thoughts mostly stayed away. Or where she was comfortable enough to fight the thoughts off, anyway.

What eventually got her to stand up was the realization that she could go to her family, and maybe even curl up in her own bed, if it still existed. Well, that and the fact that everyone was leaving, and she didn't want to stay in the school's bunker all on her own.

Thankfully, the officers from the Interkingdom Department of Crimes and Stuff were not going to apprehend everyone involved in the heist on the spot. Shmebecca, Shmayden, and Shmelix would be allowed to go home and await a summons to a local magistrate, who would then give them a sentence. Since the heist had failed, it was probably going to be a light one. Joviala tended to look at consequences, not intent.

For Bobert, Jennizabeth, and Stanbert, it was another story. They were going to be escorted through town with a big sign above them that read UP TO NO GOOD! before being put on a boat back to Nefaria, where they'd await both an interkingdom trial and a Nefarian one. That is, if there was still a town for them to march through, still a boat for them to board, still a kingdom for them to cross.

Shmebecca had caught snippets of all this in her nearly comatose state, but she hadn't been able to feel any worse than she already did. At least that's what she'd thought. Now that she was following the Nefarians, seeing their pallid expressions, she wanted to crawl back under the blankets for a long, long time.

Outside, it took a minute for her to adjust to the daylight. The sun was filtered through a thick haze of smoke and ash, but it was still much brighter than the artificial magic lights they'd been living with for the last few days.

The hole in the ground formerly known as Mount Saint Helenhunt was still active, billowing smoke, spewing out piping-hot magma (a.k.a. mountain juice), and shooting lava bombs into the air. But it was doing it a little less intensely than at the beginning, and there was hope that they'd seen the worst of it, though no one was willing to guarantee that.

A storm had rolled in a day after the mountain was destroyed, and it had helped contain the damage from the fires and clear out the worst of the air-quality concerns. The Jovialese government had sent word around town that it was reasonably safe to leave shelters for the next twelve hours to reconnect with family and gather supplies, but that all should do so on high alert. There would also be an emergency town hall that evening, barring any further major eruptions.

When Shmebecca's eyes had stopped hurting from the brightness of the day, she took in the sight around her. The school itself hadn't sustained much damage, though fires had scorched through a lot of the trees in the area. In the distance, dozens of plumes of white smoke rose into the hazy sky from fires that had been put out already.

Visibility wasn't great, so she couldn't see the gap in the mountains where her mountain used to be. Not that she really wanted to see it. She wondered briefly where they'd plopped it down, what they'd done with it. Had they started blowing it to bits to use the rocks and minerals it was composed of for some other purpose? To build the stupid amusement park, maybe? Or had they sold it off to some other kingdom?

Shmebecca wasn't sure she wanted to know.

The adults were gathering the students into several groups that could be chaperoned to different parts of town in order to be reunited with their families. Mr. Gigglebutt was following Officer KittyKat, who was escorting Bobert, Stanbert, and Jennizabeth. The plan was to have the Nefarians pick up their belongings and then travel home as soon as possible, but a lot of boats had been damaged during the volcanic event, and many more had already left.

"Where is Candelabra?" Mr. Gigglebutt asked, looking around at the Jovialese kids nearby, trying to spot her in the crowd.

"She wasn't at school when it happened," Bobert said softly.

"Is she not in trouble like the rest of you?" Mr. Gigglebutt asked.

THE GREATEST HEIST IN JOVIALA

When none of them responded, he looked at the officer, who just shook his head. "Strange," Mr. Gigglebutt added. "I would have guessed she'd be the first one to get caught up in some hijinks."

Even though she was angry at Candelabra, Shmebecca hoped that nothing bad had happened to her. Especially once they crossed through town and saw the damage.

Every window had been shattered, and there were holes in buildings where rocks had shot through. In another land, there might not have been any buildings left standing at all. It was only thanks to Jovialese disaster preparedness that the town had withstood the eruption. But this was worse than anything Shmebecca had seen before, even in textbooks describing some of the worst disasters in Jovialese history (worse than the Great Shark Tsunami, which her grandparents had lived through and never seemed to shut up about).

There were dusty people calling out loved ones' names, and crews searching through the rubble of the few buildings that hadn't been able to withstand the onslaught of fire and smoke and earthquakes, which were still rattling the ground every fifteen minutes or so.

There were fallen trees, and large cracks in the earth that seemed to give way to bottomless pits. Thunder echoed through the valley from the passing storm, and lightning was coming either from the clouds or from the eruption site, or both.

Even for a land of disasters, things looked dire. Two kids with sooty faces passed by—the older one, a teenager, looked dazed and was holding hands with a little girl about Shmorris and Shborris's age, who was crying quietly and clutching a plush toy of a warrior, one that looked surprisingly like Miss Petunias.

"Do you think Candelabra is okay?" Shmebecca asked, chewing on her lip. She wasn't sure if any of the Nefarians even wanted to talk to her. Candelabra might have betrayed the whole kingdom, but Shmebecca still didn't want Candelabra to have been caught up in whatever had been happening on the surface over the past few days.

"Even though she did a very stupid thing, she's smart," Bobert said. "I'm sure she found some shelter in time. She might even be with your parents."

But when they got to Shmebecca's house to get Bobert's things, Candelabra wasn't there. Shmebecca was thrilled to see that her parents and brothers were doing okay, and that their house had been mostly unscathed (though the tree house her dad had built a few years ago had caught fire). After a reuniting embrace, Shmebecca asked about Candelabra. Her parents frowned and said they'd assumed she was with them at school.

At that moment, Officer KittyKat knocked on the door. "Emergency town hall has been called for tonight. You and the Nefarians can stay and gather your things until then." He

THE GREATEST HEIST IN JOVIALA

looked to Bobert. "You'll say goodbye and be extradited after the town hall." He turned to leave, then paused and doubled back. "As long as there's still a Joviala to be extradited from."

For the rest of the day until the emergency town hall, Shmebecca felt a bubbling of worry and guilt in her stomach. She should have at least made sure that Candelabra wasn't on her own. Maybe she'd gotten lost on the way to school and hadn't been able to find any shelter before the eruption.

Hopefully, they would see her at the town hall, safe and sound.

That was easier said than done. This town hall wasn't like the other one she'd brought the Nefarians to. There were still snacks, a band playing pleasant music in the corner, and a generally civic vibe, despite the circumstances. People weren't yelling at one another, which still seemed to surprise the Nefarian kids. The more they talked about their kingdom, the more she wanted to visit and see what it was really like. She was jealous of the kids who'd gone to Nefaria on the student exchange that year. For many reasons. Maybe next year—if she made it to next year—she'd sign up for the program instead of being a host.

Anyway, the town hall was more crowded than any Shmebecca had ever seen. There were people who had clearly just now reunited, hugging and shedding happy tears. Some were excitedly recounting where they were when the eruption began, reliving the moment over and over again in order to process it. Some were reenacting the event by performing an interpretive dance, which Shmebecca felt was odd, though she supposed everyone was entitled to process traumatic events however they needed to.

She was surprised by how eagerly she was scanning the crowd for Candelabra's golden hair. After her family had found seats, she and Bobert split up to take a lap around the crowded auditorium. Only after about five minutes of this did she notice the looks that followed her, the whispers. They weren't judgmental looks, or condescending ones, the way they might have been after her speech warning everyone. That felt like so long ago.

But it seemed that the people in town had not forgotten what she'd said. Because the looks in their eyes, unless she was imagining them, were apologetic. A few people even said they were sorry. Shmebecca offered little smiles at these people, a flurry of confusing feelings swirling within her. There was pride, mixed with an *I told you so*-flavored resentment, mixed with worry for Candelabra, mixed with sadness for her mountain and what her home had become without it, mixed with anger at Candelabra for her hand in all of it.

After fifteen minutes of searching, she and Bobert met back up with her parents. The whole audience gasped as a rumbling filled the auditorium, but it was just someone dragging a podium up to the stage for Mayor Shmayor.

The restless crowd tried to quiet down, but the murmurs persisted until she tapped on the microphone (still just a magically enhanced can of beans) and cleared her throat.

"Good evening, everyone. Even in difficult times—especially in difficult times—it is a joy to be here with you." Shmebecca felt she did a good job saying it in a slightly sad way. She went on with some practical announcements about what to do if your home was destroyed, and the hotels or houses that were available for people who'd been displaced. She assured everyone that they would have food and shelter.

Even though that seemed like a commonsense thing for the government to provide, Shmebecca heard Bobert utter a choked-up "Wow, that's great" beside her.

Mayor Shmayor continued with some more information about where to find help, what shelters were open for those who needed them, and a reminder of some volcanic-eruption safety tips. Which made Shmebecca want to scream a little, but she knew that wouldn't undo anything, so there was no point in screaming. It wouldn't bring back her mountain.

"To that point," the mayor said, clearing her throat. She scanned the audience for a moment, and maybe Shmebecca was imagining things, but it seemed like Mayor Shmayor was looking straight at her. "There was one person who warned us that this might happen. One person who tried to save us. And I think we owe her an apology."

Now everyone in the room turned to look at her. And it was her, without a doubt, not anyone else. Shmebecca felt her cheeks redden. She didn't know what to do. Wave? That'd be weird. Smiling, too, felt like the wrong move. Maybe she should stand and curtsy?

She felt her dad's hand on her back, rubbing encouragingly. Beside her, Bobert offered a big smile. Before she knew it, the whole room was clapping for her. At first it made her proud of herself. It felt good. Redeeming. The acknowledgment that she'd been right was something she hadn't known she needed, but she did.

Then it just made her angry. Especially when she spotted Mr. Eyebrows walking through the door and joining in on the clapping.

28

SHMEBECCA STOOD UP, BREATHING VERY INTENTLY IN through her nose and out through her mouth so that smoke wouldn't start steaming out of her ears (she'd have to look up later whether that could actually happen).

This made the applause just grow louder and go on longer. So Shmebecca had to patiently wait for it to die down. When it did, the mayor nodded and was about to speak again, but Shmebecca raised her voice to carry across the room. "I'd like to say something."

"Oh," the mayor said. She looked away from the stage to one of her advisors, who shrugged.

The other interkingdom officer, PuppyChow, was standing nearby, and he cleared his throat. "With all due respect, ma'am, this child broke interkingdom law. I don't think she should be given a platform. Especially since she was the mastermind."

The mayor nodded, considering. After a while she spoke, looking back toward Shmebecca. "Yes, but if she'd gotten away with it, we might not be in this position. I doubt she'll be breaking any laws from the stage. Let's hear what she has to say." She waved Shmebecca over.

Outside, there was a boom, and everyone in the room gasped and held their breath. But someone near a window called out that it was just an arriving boat bumping into the dock. Everyone laughed at their own jumpiness.

By the time they all quieted down, Shmebecca had made her way onstage and had taken the enchanted can of beans from the mayor. She raised it to her mouth to start speaking, but hadn't thought of how to start. She stared across the room and locked eyes with Mr. Eyebrows's stupid mustached face. It was tempting to just point at him and say, "You!" She could stretch it out and make her voice all low and growly, so that he would know he was in trouble.

She could tell him this was all his fault, tell him he was a bad person who'd caused irreparable harm, and that he should be forced to leave Joviala. And it might have felt satisfying to do that. But she didn't actually care about Mr. Eyebrows. Plus, she had made her own mistakes.

Someone in the front row cleared their throat uncomfortably, and when she scanned the audience, she could tell they were worried that her speech would be a repeat of last time. Further back, her parents avoided giving embarrassing thumbs-ups, at least. Bobert locked eyes with her. She wanted him to grin his goofy grin, maybe give her a thumbs-up. He didn't do that, but he did give her a small nod.

Finally, she raised the can to address the crowd. "I made some friends this past week. They're from Nefaria, which we all know is a place famous for its evil schemes. I was a little nervous to meet them." She stopped herself. "No, actually, that's not true. I didn't care about them at first. I was too busy enjoying my time on my mountain. I wrote them off because I assumed that coming from an evil land means you're either evil, you're okay with evil, or you're probably just a jerk and don't even know it. I was more concerned with rocks, with the exciting idea that the ancient mountain that I liked to spend my time on—the mountain that once saved my life—would someday erupt." She laughed at herself. "Little did I know."

The audience laughed with her and waited for her to continue. She paced on the stage, trying to gather her thoughts. "To be honest, I'm not very good at being Jovialese. I don't smile as much as everyone else does. I can be obsessive about things that can go wrong. Although, I guess you could say it's very Jovialese to have trouble letting go." The audience chuckled along with her. But another room-shaking boom reminded her that she should hurry things along.

"The Nefarians believed me before anyone else did that

there was something going on in the mountain that needed attention. That the mountain needed rescuing. Even though they barely knew me, they were ready to help right away.

"Here in Joviala, we don't deal with evil schemes. At least not the way people usually think of them." Now she looked pointedly at Mr. Eyebrows, who at least had the decency to seem embarrassed. "But every land has a different kind of evil: ignoring the damage we cause when we seek our own interests without caring about who gets hurt is its own kind of evil."

She took a deep breath, readying herself to say what she had to say. She hadn't even known that she needed to until she'd arrived on the stage and looked out at the audience. At Bobert and his kind expression, at Stanbert all stone-faced and sleep-deprived, at Jennizabeth's red-rimmed eyes. Officer KittyKat stood beside them, arms crossed over his big chest, ready to take them back home. Shmebecca had known about the consequences, and yet she had dragged them into this and tried to make it seem like everything was going to be okay. Because she knew it likely would be—for her.

"I don't know if Mr. Eyebrows intended to cause all this harm. I don't think he did, actually. The Fun Corporation has a history of this: being careless while going after what they want. Whatever it was the Fun Corporation wanted, it wasn't this." She gestured outside, where at that moment there was an orange flash. The mountain was helping her make her point, even if it was gone. "An amusement park would be great. Lasagnanite and the riches it could bring Joviala, sure, awesome. But look at the costs. *Before* something happens, not after.

"I know we're all proud of being Jovialese. Of our capacity to survive disaster." Again she gestured at the outside world, garnering a good chuckle from the crowd. She noticed the door to the auditorium cracking open and then closing as someone shut it softly behind them, not wanting to interrupt. She couldn't tell who it was, but she caught a glimpse of golden hair.

"We have these strong fingers that we use to protect ourselves and hang on to what's important to us. We use them for the fun of booger-flicking contests and mountain climbing, and to catch rides on rat-birds without falling off them as they speed through the air. But we have to be able to let go of certain things too. Including our belief that nothing can go wrong here." She swallowed, the sound echoing throughout the room thanks to the can of beans. "In that sense, I've been very Jovialese." She looked at Bobert and the others, wishing that Candelabra were there to hear this too, despite it all. "I'm sorry that I lied to you. I was just thinking of what I wanted to happen instead of what could potentially go wrong for you. You helped me, and you deserved better than how I treated you. I'm sorry."

Shmebecca lowered the can of beans. She'd said all she'd

needed to. The speech was maybe just as rambling as her first one, but this time everyone in the audience had been listening. They were nodding along. Some were even wiping at their eyes. Though that could have been because of everything they'd lived through in the last three days. The door in the back of the room opened again, and there were some murmurs as a few latecomers made their way in, along with a few ensuing shushes.

Since Shmebecca had wandered away from the podium, she crossed the stage again to hand the can of beans back to the mayor.

"I'd like to say something too, if I may!" a voice called out.

Shmebecca couldn't believe it. Mr. Eyebrows had raised his hand and was making his way through the crowd toward the stage.

Except he wasn't smiling anymore. It was the first time she'd seen him where half his face wasn't taken up with teeth. He seemed to pick up on the tension filling the room, because he raised his hands as he approached. "Rest assured, I am not going to push back against anything this wise, angry child has said."

Shmebecca froze. The mayor did too, each of them with a hand on the can now, looking like they were fighting for who would speak next. Even though they were both speechless. The

THE GREATEST HEIST IN JOVIALA

whole room was waiting with bated breath to see what would happen.

Mr. Eyebrows climbed up the side stairs and onto the stage, gesturing for the can. "May I?"

The mayor looked at Shmebecca. "Your call," she said in a low voice.

It would be so satisfying to shake her head. To not give Mr. Eyebrows a chance to explain himself, offer excuses, blame someone else. But there was something about him that seemed earnest, and Shmebecca wanted to take her own advice. Holding on to anger took more strength than she had. She looked over at the back of the room, noticing that there were still people streaming in, some of them wearing big, pointy hats.

She looked at the mayor and nodded, and when she handed off the can to Mr. Eyebrows, he squatted to look Shmebecca in the eyes, speaking just to her, not yet into the microphone (microcan?). "I am sorry for what I have done. And I will do what I can to make things right."

She could tell he meant the words, even if she didn't really think he had any way to make things right. So she just nodded and then moved to the side next to the mayor, letting Mr. Eyebrows say whatever he was going to say.

"There is no easy way to say this," he said, taking in a deep breath. "We at Fun Corporation are deeply regretful of the mistake that was made. Moving Mount Saint Helenhunt was . . ." He made circles with one hand, like he was searching for the word in the air and trying to beckon it into his mouth. "A disaster. It was a preventable disaster. Unfortunately, as our young friend here pointed out, it was pursued with selfish interests at heart. The dangers were ignored." Mr. Eyebrows stepped away for a second, taking a deep breath as he appeared to gather his thoughts, or his courage (if he had any). "You see, dear people of Joviala, I have a confession. I am not like you." He bowed his head and then looked up to face the crowd. "I am not Jovialese at all."

There were some murmurs from the crowd. Shmebecca felt the urge to turn to the mayor and mutter something too, but didn't want to miss what he was going to say next.

"I was born and raised in Los Angsteles, a land that I love for many reasons, but which I left for just as many reasons. And I came here to Joviala, where suddenly I was happy. You wonderful people with your big hearts and big smiles welcomed me, and showed me what it was like to live a life that wasn't spent worrying—which was a lot of my childhood in Los Angsteles. Here, though, I was free to pursue fun. I had never really discovered it until I lived here, to be honest." He smiled now, but it was a slightly sad smile, without all those teeth. It was the first smile he'd given that Shmebecca felt was a real one. "I have become single-minded in my pursuit of fun.

This kingdom gave it to me, and I wanted to return the favor."

Now it wasn't just his smile becoming more real, but his voice, too. Shmebecca felt herself believing him, caring about what he was saying, her defenses dropping. Part of her hated that.

"This is all coming across as me trying to excuse myself," Mr. Eyebrows continued, twirling the left side of his mustache absentmindedly. "Rest assured, I am only trying to explain. We at the Fun Corporation are deeply regretful of our error. Of my error. And we are committing ourselves to fixing the damage we have caused. However we can."

"So tell us how!" someone shouted. Shmebecca looked in their direction and saw that it was her mom, her brow furrowed in anger, her arms crossed over her chest. "Or better yet, do it."

The audience murmured its agreement. An earthquake was starting up, but it felt like it would be a small one, and though a few people covered their heads with their arms, no one seemed to mind the shaking very much.

"We will be granting one free entry to the amusement park to every person in Joviala!" He smiled his big fake smile again and seemed to be waiting for applause. Instead there was stunned silence, followed by a scattering of boos. Mr. Eyebrows took a deep breath. "Yes, Shmindy told me it was too soon to mention that. Old habits." He sucked his teeth. "Okay, how about one free entry and one free child-sized beverage of your choosing?" More boos followed. "Keep in mind that this isn't a beverage whose size is appropriate for children. It is a beverage cup the size of an average five-year old human." He held his hands in the air and clapped for himself, clearly wanting everyone else to follow along.

"Shut up about the park!" someone from the crowd yelled. "Fix the problem!"

"Right," Mr. Eyebrows said, bowing his head. "Unfortunately, the Muffin of Glory was damaged during the eruption. So . . . other than continuing with planned construction of the amusement park once all this chaos is over, we're not quite sure what to do." He dabbed at his forehead, where sweat was starting to glisten and drip. "I'd like to add that we are consulting with volcanologists. Please clap."

A deep silence fell over the town hall. Shmebecca felt she would have been able to hear her heart drop, if it hadn't already. She'd lost hope sometime in the past three days. It seemed, though, that a lot of the people in town hadn't yet, and were not ready to hear what Mr. Eyebrows had said.

The room erupted with the sound of people screaming questions. Chairs scraped back against the floor as people stood to yell, and some to leave, perhaps headed straight to the docks to escape the land now that there was no solution in sight. Even the mayor, who'd been standing calmly beside

Shmebecca, took a step forward and addressed Mr. Eyebrows. "Do you mean to say you don't have any way to move the mountain back? Maybe that will solve it."

Through all the noise, Shmebecca heard a distinctive whistle. It was coming from the back of the room, where the pointy hats had gathered, so many of them that Shmebecca could no longer see the golden hair that had called out to her.

It seemed that no one else had heard the whistle, though, until it rang out again, this time twice as loud, cutting through the noise. If there were still windows left anywhere in town, some would surely have shattered.

The whole room returned to silence, looking back toward the door. There stood Imogene Petunias. She was standing next to Officer PuppyChow. She pulled out the two fingers from her mouth that she'd used to whistle. "Sorry to interrupt," she called out, not needing a microphone to project to the entire room. "But there's someone here who may have an idea for you."

She stepped aside, revealing Candelabra and a woman who looked a lot like her. Shmebecca couldn't deny that anger was still there upon seeing her former temporary sister. But there was a great amount of relief, too.

"I brought some friends with me," Candelabra said, projecting as loudly as she could while gesturing at the various bearded people in pointy hats around her. "And I think they can help."

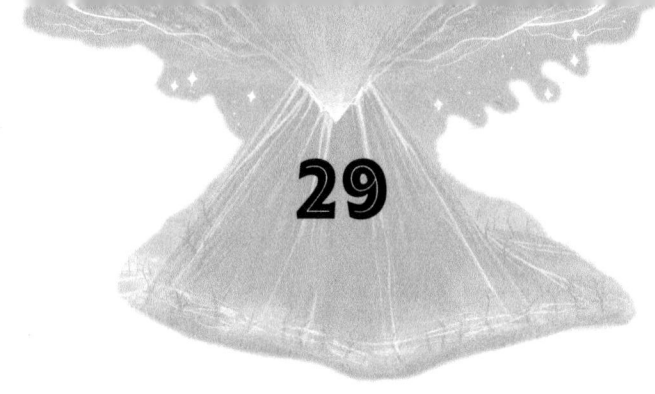

29

FOR THE PAST FEW DAYS CANDELABRA HAD BEEN HEARING the news coming from Joviala, worried to death about her friends, about the place she'd been responsible for destroying. She'd spent hours talking with Sandraliere, trying to find a solution. Even though Sandraliere could have left her side to do any one of the dozens of things she hadn't been able to do in the painting—visit friends, go for a run in the mountains, spend a whole day in a museum—she stayed.

Finally, Candelabra had remembered overhearing Bobert telling Shmebecca about the volcanic-stabilizing spell that Mr. Gigglebutt had told him about. So Candelabra and Sandraliere had put out word that they were in need of wizards. Thankfully, a lot of bureaucracy had changed in Nefaria since the kingdom was briefly ruled by Matt the Wizard the year before, and now it didn't take so long to invoke emergency procedures.

The wizards had spread the word themselves, the Nefarian government had chartered a ship, and now here they all were, ready to help. All they had to do was arrive safely at the site of the eruption.

The attitude at the town hall was pretty much *What are we waiting for?* Which was also what Candelabra shouted from the door. Almost as soon as Candelabra announced that there were twenty wizards standing by, ready to save Joviala, everyone started filing out.

Once most of the people had left, Bobert came running at her. She braced herself for the tirade that he would unleash, which she deserved. Instead he wrapped her up in a hug. "I'm sorry I was so harsh. I knew you'd do the right thing," he said.

She tried to keep herself from crying, because if she started again she might not stop, and they needed to go save a kingdom. "I'm sorry," she said simply.

"I know you are. But you came back." He squeezed again, then pulled away. "Did I just see Matt the freaking Evil Wizard here?"

"Yeah. He wanted to help, and the Council of Elders gave him a temporary pass, since it's for a good cause."

"Is that a good idea?"

"I guess we'll see. He doesn't seem as fired up anymore, and he looked serious about wanting to help. He said something about learning to seek approval from others in less dramatic and dangerous ways. We'll just have to make sure he doesn't go near any more gumball machines."

Bobert laughed and looked over his shoulder, where Shmebecca was standing. She didn't look like she wanted to punch Candelabra, so that was good. Although Candelabra would have taken a punch if it would help Shmebecca know how sorry she was.

"I'm gonna go meet your sister," Bobert said, gesturing to Sandraliere, who was at the snack table, sampling everything that was laid out.

Now Candelabra waited for Shmebecca to step forward. She wanted to say she was sorry another seven thousand times, give or take. But she knew that sometimes saying sorry wasn't enough. It could actually be annoying to the person you'd hurt, unless you *showed* that you were sorry and were willing to correct your error. Which was why she was here.

Somehow, Shmebecca seemed to be on this exact same page. She didn't hug Candelabra, but she did say that she was happy Candy was okay. The town hall was almost empty now: the voices that had been filling the space were now chattering outside, getting farther away as they began the march toward the former site of the mountain.

"Thanks for coming back," Shmebecca said. "I am upset that you ruined the greatest heist Joviala has ever seen, but I'm glad you're here, and I understand why you did it. I wish you hadn't. But I understand. And for what it's worth, I'm sorry too. I should have been clear about what could happen to you and your friends if we failed. I'm gonna do everything I can to make sure they're okay. Even if it means breaking you out of some Nefarian jail. I'll do it."

Candelabra nodded, wiping a tear that was slipping from the corner of her eye. "I guess, if nothing else, we learned we'd make a really good team of thieves."

Shmebecca laughed. "Stanbert still hasn't shut up about how he should be involved in more heists. We were literally hiding in a bunker for three days because our last one failed, and he's already planning his future as a criminal mastermind."

They laughed, and then, when it seemed nothing more needed to be said between them, they called out to Bobert and Sandraliere that it was time to go save the kingdom.

It had started raining, which was preferable for the safety of everyone who came. That turned out to be almost everyone in town. The fires around the mountain hole had mostly fizzled out, and the wet earth kept new ones from getting too unwieldy.

The bystanders stayed near the tree line, not far from the river that had been the contingency plan for getting rid of the Muffin of Glory. Most of the crowd wore cloths around their faces to keep from breathing in smoke, but almost no one bothered to shelter themselves from the rain. After three days indoors hiding from the elements, it felt good to be exposed to them without fear. Or at least not *that* much fear—there were still occasional explosions of magma and rocks and thick black smoke.

The wizards were much closer to the mountain site, since they needed the magic to be as strong as possible. Their colored robes flapped in the wind, as did their beards, which every single wizard had, regardless of gender. Thankfully, the wind was blowing away from them, so the toxic plumes of smoke only caused a few of the wizards to pass out as they were getting ready to cast the spell. The crowd gasped as those wizards fainted, after which the other wizards nearby would pause to point their wands at the fallen wizards and wake them back up.

Matt, one-time king of Nefaria as well as Chillest Wizard and Master of Blizzards (among many other nicknames no one had ever heard anyone but Matt use), tried to give a rallying speech to the other wizards before they began casting the spell. But Bobert and Candelabra knew that it was best not to let him go on too long, because he might fire himself up in the wrong ways and then try to steal the mountain for himself or something. Even this new, somewhat rehabilitated version of the wizard could cause a lot of unintended damage. They waved to him as a distraction, knowing he wouldn't be able to resist waving back enthusiastically.

THE GREATEST HEIST IN JOVIALA

Now, standing about ten feet apart from each other, the wizards all pointed their wands at where Mount Saint Helenhunt used to stand.

The witnessing Nefarians felt a sense of déjà vu. They hadn't experienced anything specifically like this, of course, but the act of holding their breath and seeing if good would prevail, if a bunch of people holding sticks could change the course of fate—that felt strangely familiar.

The Jovialese witnesses were less used to the worry bubbling within them. They were well acquainted with the destruction the land could unleash on them. But they weren't used to being able to stop it. It was a strange feeling of power and hope, even if they weren't the ones holding the wands.

Bobert, Candelabra, and Shmebecca stood side by side at the front of the crowd, along with the rest of their crew. Miss Petunias was there too, arms crossed over her chest, looking around protectively.

Purple lightning streaked through the cloud emanating from the hole; then thunder rumbled, so loud it seemed to crack the earth—though the earth had plenty of cracks in it already. A spurt of magma shot out from one of them, fanning out dangerously toward the wizards. A young female wizard in teal robes (and a matching teal beard) waved her wand and the magma turned into small orange birds in midair, chirping as they flew over the heads of the crowd, who oohed with delight.

"It's time, you fools!" Matt's gravelly voice shouted at the other wizards. And even though everyone rolled their eyes, they began chanting together.

They were not perfectly in sync, though, which was crucial for the volcanic-stabilizing spell. A few wizards were chanting too quickly, and a tall, gangly wizard near Matt was using a cadence more suited to slam poetry. So they started over.

Again, someone was a half step too slow.

Which made sense: they hadn't had time to rehearse, and they were from at least four different kingdoms, which made coordination a little more difficult. Finally, one of the wizards started a countdown—which was interrupted by someone asking, "Are we starting *on* three, or *after*?"—and then finally their voices were perfectly matched.

Another explosion echoed across the valley as a large rock came barreling out from the clouds toward the crowd. The wizards continued with their chanting, but many in the crowd let out a scream and started scrambling.

Shmebecca, Bobert, and Candelabra all shuffled backward, not wanting to look away from the spell casting but trying to track the rock's movement at the same time. It seemed to be headed straight for the crowd, until another rock came flying toward it and knocked it out of the air.

Imogene Petunias had somehow grabbed a rock the size of

a small child and tossed it more than a hundred feet in the air to save the crowd. Both rocks fell harmlessly to the ground in the field between the wizards and the audience.

The crowd cheered, but the mountain hole wasn't done making things difficult. Maybe they—the wizards with their wands, or the Fun Corporation with its recklessness, or all the people of Joviala with their hubris—had awakened it. Or maybe it was always going to do this, and it *seemed* like it was fighting them. This was just nature, responding. It didn't see them as an enemy at all. Either way, the ground started shaking, and another huge crack started forming. It was racing out straight toward them, as if some invisible monster had sunk its fingers into the ground and was trying to tear the earth in two.

More magma and smoke came flowing out of the crack, and one of the wizards had to throw themself to the side to avoid falling in, though they managed to keep their wand pointed at the right place and were still speaking the words for the spell.

A few more lava bombs shot out toward the crowd, and even Miss Petunias couldn't stop them all. She knocked a couple more out of the air, and Bobert, bless his little heart, tried as well. But he could barely lift a rock big enough to stop one of the projectiles, much less toss it far enough into the air. He did find a pebble and throw it pretty far, but his aim was off and he almost hit Matt the Wizard in the side of the face.

"They're not going to make it in time," Shmebecca said, frozen in place. A small fire had started about thirty feet from where she was standing, but she was oblivious, eyes glued to the wizards. "It's going to explode. Even more."

She wanted to warn everyone around her, but even those already running didn't stand a chance. If it was going to happen, nothing nearby was going to survive.

Then a soft green light started forming at the tips of the wizards' wands. Just as soon as the doom had nestled into Shmebecca's heart, this green glow made her feel like there was hope. However, the crack in the earth was spreading, almost like it was running straight to her. *You always wanted to be a part of this mountain,* it seemed to be saying. *Here's your chance.*

More fire, more lava, more smoke. Shmebecca's eyes started to water; her breath burned in her lungs. It was too late, she thought. Not only was her mountain gone, but her whole town would soon disappear too. The wizards had arrived too late, or the damage the Fun Corporation had unleashed on Joviala was too much to reverse. There was another boom, and Shmebecca saw that yet another crack in the ground was forming, and it, too was spreading in her direction, like a snake rushing toward a helpless mouse.

Then she hit the ground hard. Dazed, she noticed that

Candelabra was on top of her, looking bruised and sheepish. They both looked back at the place where they'd been standing moments earlier and saw that it had split completely in two. Shmebecca would have been swallowed up if Candelabra hadn't tackled her to the ground.

"Thanks," Shmebecca managed to say, catching her breath from the impact.

"Any time," Candelabra said. She brushed herself off, then reached a hand out to help Shmebecca up.

There were so many explosions happening, it sounded like fireworks or war (even though Joviala didn't actually have either, and Shmebecca had only learned about them from reading books). People were screaming, calling out for one another; the ground was shaking, the air unbreathable. One man wearing three helmets stacked on top of one another was running in circles, yelling about how they were all going to die or at least get really hurt. In short: chaos.

Now Bobert was standing over both Shmebecca and Candelabra. "Look!" he screamed. And somehow he had a smile on his face. *What a weird, happy kid,* Shmebecca found herself thinking.

She'd gotten turned around on the fall, but now she saw that Bobert was pointing at the wizards, and at the hole where her mountain used to be. Her poor mountain.

But the green light was not just a slight glow anymore.

It was a full globe, and it was encapsulating . . . well, it was hard to tell how big it was because of all the smoke. But if Shmebecca had to guess, she'd say that the green globe was the size of Mount Saint Helenhunt.

There was another boom—not as loud, though, as if someone had suddenly turned down the volume or moved the explosions farther away. Shmebecca wasn't sure if the explosion was smaller, or if the globe of light had something to do with it. Were the wizards done? She rose to her feet, a little shaky, even though the ground itself wasn't to blame for once.

The wizards were still pointing their wands, but it seemed like they were done reciting the spell. She could hear their voices for the first time in what felt like hours, though it had probably been ten minutes at most. Every now and then there was a scream from somewhere nearby, or a sob. But slowly the volume decreased on *all* the chaos.

There were no more booms. None of the terrifying whooshes that had come with the earth splitting in two. No more thuds of rocks hitting the ground, no more crackling of fire.

Finally: silence.

It wasn't clear right away, but once the people who were gathered at the site formerly known as Mount Saint Helenhunt picked up on what they were hearing (or not hearing), they stopped running. They stopped praying and calling out to one another. Instead they just stared at the place that used to be a mountain, and had then become a series of natural disasters, but was now still.

It was smoky, and lava-y, and it looked like it had suffered many explosions, yes. But it was still.

The nightmare that had ruled Joviala for a few days, the nightmare that Shmebecca had been trying all along to stop, was over.

30

THE LAST THING THAT THE VISITING CHILDREN OF NEFARIA learned about the people of Joviala was that they knew how to celebrate. They knew how to breathe a sigh of relief and party when they'd escaped disaster unscathed.

Since there was no more danger, the Nefarians did not return home early. They stayed in Joviala one more day, as originally planned. Officers KittyKat and PuppyChow, after being in communication with the Interkingdom Department of Crimes and Stuff, declared that, due to Acts of Extraordinary Bravery, and also Being Right About Stuff, the kids involved in the heist would have their charges dropped.

In celebration, they feasted on local snacks (many of which they hadn't encountered during all their touring around). They listened to local music, and watched the locals dance, then clumsily tried to imitate those dances.

The Fun Corporation funded it all. This was in addition to funding the town's cleanup and the maintenance required for the volcanic-stabilizing spell (most of that went toward a wizard's retainer fee). The cost bankrupted the company, which absolutely no one was sad about. Not even Mr. Eyebrows, who was too busy having fun to appreciate that his PR stunt had ended the corporation he had started.

The morning before they were set to return, Bobert, Candelabra, Stanbert, and Jennizabeth walked with Shmebecca, Shmayden, and Shmelix to the site of the mountain.

Not the site where the mountain used to be, since there were still some lingering toxic fumes there, and too many workers milling about, cleaning stuff up and running heavy machinery.

No, they went to the new resting place for Mount Saint Helenhunt. It was a few miles away, in a prairie that had no business hosting a mountain of that size. Geologically, it made no sense. But it was still there. Her mountain. It wasn't a volcano anymore, not really. That part of it belonged to the old site, which even now was forming a new mountain above it. But Shmebecca still had it, and she didn't care whether it was technically just a really big pile of rocks. She hadn't lost it at all. It had saved her life and then she had saved it back. Sort of.

"I kind of like it here," Bobert said, staring up at it, craning his head sideways. The moving crew hadn't set it down all that carefully, laying it on uneven ground, so its peak was slightly tilted. "It suits the mountain."

"I have no idea what he's talking about," Stanbert said. "It doesn't belong here."

Shmebecca laughed, shrugging her shoulders. "I don't care. I'm just happy it still exists."

For the next hour they all searched for rocks to add to Shmebecca's mosaic. They joked about their heist, laughing at how Stanbert had rolled around on the floor trying to tie the guards' shoelaces, and how Shmebecca hadn't known how to use the sleeping powder and almost made them all fall asleep before the heist could even really start.

They slowly added pieces to the new mini Mount Saint Helenhunt, and now that it wasn't just her, now that she had the help of all these other kids, they finished the project before the Nefarians had to catch their boat home. Throughout this time, though, what Stanbert had said about the mountain not belonging there stuck with her.

"I'm going to miss you guys," Shmebecca told them on the walk to the dock, her mind still churning.

"Not all of us, I'm sure," Candelabra said, exaggerating her tone in a way that made it sound like she was joking, even though it was clear that she wasn't joking entirely.

"All of you," Shmebecca insisted.

"Even those who were part of an evil scheme?"

"Look, nobody's perfect," Shmebecca said. "I should know."

They arrived at the dock, where some of Shmebecca's class-

THE GREATEST HEIST IN JOVIALA

mates had arrived to bid the Nefarians goodbye. They waved, and some cried, and a few rushed over to offer hugs. There were other travelers from Nefaria, too, who were to board the same boat home. A few were sprinting onto the ship, eager to get back to a land where they only had to worry about kooky wizards trying to put them in armor or something, instead of the world itself trying to kill them.

Miss Petunias was standing by the boat, and she waved at the group, then pointed at her wrist to tell them they had to hurry. *What an odd gesture,* Shmebecca thought. Joviala was a land without wristwatches.

Bobert took a deep breath, and everyone could tell he was trying not to cry, even if the tears he was avoiding would be happy ones. "I just need to enjoy this perfect weather a little longer," he said, closing his eyes and pointing his face toward the sun.

They all joined him for a moment. It was almost unbelievably nice. Not just the weather, but being able to notice the weather. To have the luxury of closing your eyes and feeling the sun on your skin and the breeze in your hair.

When they opened their eyes again, Shmebecca took off her backpack and pulled out the mosaic. "I want you all to have this."

"What? No! We can't take that. You've been working on it forever," Jennizabeth said, eyes wide.

Shmebecca ignored her, walked forward, and put the mosaic in Candelabra's hands.

"Are you sure?" her former host-sister and new friend asked.

Shmebecca didn't hesitate to nod. "Thanks to you, I still have my mountain. You can have this one to remember me by."

"Last call for Nefaria!" Miss Petunias yelled out, her booming voice carrying easily across the dock.

All the kids turned to look at her, and laughed as Mr. Gigglebutt ran on board, holding his hat to his head, as if they would really leave without him when he'd been standing just a few feet away.

Miss Petunias looked at them and nodded her head toward the boat. It was really time to go. The kids all looked at one another solemnly, like in a staring contest but one where the participants were trying not to be the first to cry. Then they realized they didn't care if they lost that particular contest, and they all started crying at the same time.

They formed a tight group hug, the kind that can only be formed by people who are happy to have survived something together.

Whether what they had survived was evil or natural, or some mix of the two, it didn't quite matter. They had survived.

"One last thing before you go," Shmebecca said, pulling away from the group hug. "I think I agree with Stanbert."

THE GREATEST HEIST IN JOVIALA

"There's a first time for everything," Jennizabeth said.

"Hey!"

They all laughed; then Candelabra asked what Shmebecca meant.

She bit her lip, knowing that a twinkle was in her eye. "What he said about the mountain being in the wrong place." It was a ridiculous thought, she knew. But she'd had more ridiculous ones. "Maybe we should get the team together again sometime," Shmebecca said. "We didn't *technically* pull off the greatest heist in Joviala—but I think we have it in us."

"Oh good," Stanbert exclaimed. "I wasn't actually ready to retire."

They all laughed just as the boat's horn blared its final warning. Even if the boat was going to take them back to a land of evil schemes, Nefaria was home. And it was time to go home.

ACKNOWLEDGMENTS

Thank you to every single person involved in helping make this book a reality. That includes but is not limited to: Pete Knapp, Stuti Telidevara, Jessi Smith, Kristina Kister, Laura Lyn DiSiena, Karen Sherman, Irene Vandervoort, and many more people at Aladdin and Park & Fine who work behind the scenes to make it all happen.

I couldn't do this without regular childcare provided by Gaby Luna and Sally Fairbank. And my parents when they can (I know they wish they could more).

The more of these I write, the longer the list of names should be, and the less it feels like a list of names suffices. I'm thankful to the many readers, teachers, librarians, and booksellers, who have kept me in the book world for over a decade now.

To my family as always. To Laura Fairbank, for watching silly movies with me and always indulging me in how a certain situation could be improved with a heist. To Remy for existing. Yonce for keeping me company on late night writing sessions.

And to The Freeze, whose treats powered me through an intense summer of writing. Rest in (Reese's) peaces (sorry).

ABOUT THE AUTHOR

Born and raised in Mexico City, **ADI ALSAID** is the author of several young adult novels including *Let's Get Lost*, *We Didn't Ask for This*, and *North of Happy*, a *Kirkus* Best Book nominee. He currently lives in Chicago with his wife, son, and cat, where he occasionally spills hot sauce on things and cats (but at the time of this writing, not yet on his son). Visit Adi at AdiAlsaid.com.